A Last Resort
for
Desperate People

A Last Resort
for
Desperate People

Short Stories and A Novella

Jeremy Griffin

STEPHEN F. AUSTIN STATE UNIVERSITY PRESS

For information, address Stephen F. Austin State University Press, 1936 North
Street, LAN 203, Nacogdoches, Texas, 75962.

Cover illustration by Sarah Dexter
Cover design by April Baker
Book design by Laura McKinney

LIBRARY OF CONGRESS CATALOGING-IN-PUBLICATION DATA

Griffin, Jeremy,
A Last Resort for Desperate People : stories and a novella / Jeremy Griffin.—1st
ed.
p. cm.
ISBN-13: 978-1-936208-48-6

I. Title

First Edition: January 2012

CONTENTS

ACKNOWLEDGMENTS

Some stories in this collection have appeared in the following publications:

"Kiss" in *Blackbird*
"Once the Queen is Gone" in *Blood Orange Review*
"The Great American Grill" in the *Greensboro Review*
"Reshma" in *Gulf Stream*
"A Last Resort for Desperate People" in *Hayden's Ferry Review*
"Inflation" in *Hot Metal Bridge*
"The Shed" in *Offcourse*

A Last Resort for Desperate People

I met Arlo Furman in the third grade when my mom had me transferred into one of the special ed classes at my school because I couldn't read or do math too well. He sat next to me at our small two-person table—we had tables instead of desks—and at recess we would compete to see who could go the highest on the swings. Of course, for Arlo there wasn't much point; at close to a hundred and fifty pounds, he was the fattest kid I'd ever known, fatter even than some adults I knew, though it wasn't really his fault. "It's my pituitary gland," was how he'd explained it to me once, wrapping his thick lips around each syllable as though he were reciting a poem. "It's overactive."

Now we were in the fifth grade, and not much had changed; we still shared a table in the musty little special ed classroom, and we still tried to outswing each other at recess. The only thing different was Arlo's weight, close to two hundred pounds by this point, a figure that seemed to fill him with a strange sort of pride.

I was eleven years old, living with my mom and my stepdad Kelly who everyone just called Joe because his name tended to confuse people who didn't know him. Our house was nestled amongst a cluster of two-story prefab jobs out on Dexter Road, a short stretch of Highway 37 that ran along the base of a large wooded ridge. A long time ago, a group of Confederate soldiers had hid up on that ridge and ambushed a bunch of Union guys on their way down to Charleston. At least that's what Joe had told me once. He'd spent two years as a history major before deciding that college wasn't really his thing. And even though none of my teachers had ever heard of this, that didn't stop me and Arlo from going hunting for old musket balls out in the woods.

Arlo lived in a dark little bungalow on the opposite side of the ridge with his mom, who was a cook at a seafood restaurant, and his dad, an ex-marine who had screwed up his spine during the Gulf War when someone tossed a grenade at his jeep and who now mostly just laid around the house, watching talk shows and collecting checks from the government. Arlo's older brother Jake, who was actually Mr. Furman's kid from a previous marriage, lived in a small apartment above the garage. He was twenty-five and did road construction for the city. Years earlier, when Arlo was still in diapers, Jake had gotten busted for selling marijuana and had spent a couple months in the juvenile correctional center in Raleigh, and even though Arlo swore that Jake was totally straightened out now, that he had just had some issues to deal with back then, you know, because his mother wasn't around anymore, my mom and Joe still weren't crazy about me hanging out over at the Furmans' house, at least not when Jake was around, even though, as they'd explained to me over dinner one night, they still thought Arlo was a very nice young man and were more than happy to have him over to our house whenever I wanted. I assured them that I didn't really like going over to Arlo's house anyway because the Furmans kind of creeped me out and because the place smelled like feet.

Instead, Arlo and I would usually meet up at this elementary school playground a little ways down the road from my house. On weekends, the older kids from the nearby neighborhoods would go out there to have sex. We knew this because every so often we would come across a used condom lying in the dirt like a swath of dead snakeskin, and one time we even found a pair of girls' underwear on the ground near the back fence. They were light blue with lace around the edges and were made from a thin material that reminded me, oddly, of the mosquito netting on my grandparents' back porch. "Hey, Kev! Look!" Arlo cackled, holding the filthy things out in front of him with two hands. I could see that the backside was caked with thick black mud. "It's like she had an accident, see?" Then, in a goofy falsetto, he whined, "*Oh no! I've ruined my pretty panties! Whatever will I dooooo?*"

From the playground we would wander off into the woods that separated mine and Arlo's neighborhoods. This was where we spent most of our time outside of school. We'd bring along the paintball guns we'd gotten for Christmas, and we would play Army Commandos, a game we'd come up with where you were supposed to get a point each time you hit your opponent, only we had quickly discovered that keeping score was too much of a hassle and so mostly we just ran around shooting at each other. All over the ridge were trees splattered with red (Arlo's) and blue (mine) paint—evidence of previous battles.

The only problem was that Arlo wasn't much of a commando. He was too slow and clumsy, always falling over and needing a minute to catch his breath, and at his size it wasn't hard to spot him hunkered down behind a tree like some big flabby bear. Plus, he made way too much noise. You could hear him from all the way across the woods practically, huffing and coughing and wheezing as he struggled up the ridge, like he'd just completed a marathon.

Lucky for him though, he was a ridiculously good shot. I don't know if it was his military genes or what, but he could plant a paintball in the middle of your chest from fifty yards away, which is not an easy thing to do, particularly when you're surrounded by trees. Of course, it helped that his gun was a top-of-the-line model with a scope and retractable stock and titanium components. Mr. Furman had picked it out, said he wasn't going to have his son going around with a piss-poor firearm, even if it did only shoot paintballs. I suspected that it was actually one of the nicest things that Arlo's family owned.

Lately, however, we'd become more interested in spying on my neighbor Gina Courtier. She and her husband Steadman had moved in a few houses down from me six months earlier. Arlo would bring the binoculars he'd snagged from his dad's closetful of old army gear and we would head up to the large fallen oak tree on the top of the ridge behind their house. Standing on the massive trunk, hidden among the thick branches, you could see straight down into the Courtiers' back yard where Gina spent most of her afternoons in a plastic patio chair, dressed in a green silk robe, reading magazines and chain smoking. And when the venetian blinds on the glass double doors at the back of the house were open, we could see right into the living room, where the only furniture appeared to be a large entertainment center and a couple of black leather couches.

From what we gathered, Steadman was the only one of them who worked. He had some high-level manager position at one of the local radio stations, a job that tended to keep him out of the house until after dark. He was a pale, gangly figure who on weekends you could spot mowing their meager square of back yard in tattered jean shorts and black socks, while his wife looked on with queenly approval. Arlo and I called him "The Alien" because of how closely he resembled the spindly humanoid creatures on the Scifi Channel. He didn't seem like an appropriate match for Gina, a thin woman with lovely salt-and-pepper hair and black horn-rimmed glasses that made her seem sophisticated and clever. As far as we could tell, she never left the house, except for the few times a week when she would head down to the Texaco for another carton of smokes.

On some level, I understood that I was attracted to Gina, although if you asked me then I probably wouldn't have said it in so many words. I sure as hell would not have admitted that I thought of her as *mysterious*, which was actually sort of my mom's doing, because she was the one who had warned me to stay away from the Courtiers' house, especially on the two Saturdays a month when the fifteen or so cars would show up at their place around seven. They would spill out of the driveway and line up along the edge of the road, all the way down to our place. On these nights, my mom would hide behind the thick green curtain in our living room and watch as the small groups of men and women climbed out of their vehicles and laughingly made their way up the road toward the Courtiers' place. "Oh, that's lovely," she would grumble at the window pane. "Leave ruts in my grass. That's just fine. I love ruts in my grass."

One night I asked her what was going on up the street. "It's like a club, Honey," she replied without looking at me.

"What kind of club?"

"One for very sick people," said Joe, who was sitting in the recliner on the other side of the room with his feet up, enjoying his semi-weekly glass of something-or-other, and I could tell from his voice that I wasn't going to get anything more than this, but I had an idea he meant the other kind of sick, the in-the-head kind.

Then one afternoon Arlo showed up at the playground and told me that Jake had explained to him what the Courtiers were up to. Apparently, Jake had a friend who did maintenance work at Steadman's radio station. "They all do it together," Arlo said with a kind of disgusted smirk. "Like, they just get naked and hang out in the living room and do it with each other."

"That's not true," I said, partly to myself. I was sitting in front of him, squished down into one of the swings. He was standing there in the sickly-looking crabgrass, holding his paintball gun by the barrel.

"Yes it is, too," he protested. "Jake says that's why they had to move out of their old house, because of all of them doing it. He says it's against the law or something."

I thought this over for a moment. "Then how come they're not in jail, if they're still doing it?"

"It's only against the law out where they used to live, is what Jake says."

Arlo's version of the story, which would later be backed up by more reliable sources, was patchy, but I knew him well enough to understand what he was trying to get across. It seemed that Gina and Steadman had gotten into some trouble with their former neighbors over their bimonthly sex parties, which they'd advertised on their website as "the premier swingers' club of the Southeast." The neighbors had complained to the city council which, in response, had passed a series of ordinances that had more or less outlawed the parties. This was what Arlo meant when he said the parties were only illegal where they used to live; Dexter Road was outside of the corporate limits, beyond the reach of the ordinances.

I had twisted myself around in the swing, winding the chains into a knot just above my head, and now I took my feet off the ground and went spinning in the opposite direction.

"That's stupid," I said.

"You don't believe me?"

"No way. You can't do it with lots of people. It has to be, like, a guy and girl."

"Jake says you can do it with as many people as you want."

"Well, Jake's a liar."

"No he isn't!" Arlo snapped, leaning in toward me a little, and I knew that I'd hit a nerve. Arlo didn't like it when you called his brother names. He looked up to Jake even more than he did to his own war-hero dad.

Almost immediately, Arlo caught himself and with a frustrated sigh, he said, "He didn't make it up, Kev, okay? His friend told him."

I wanted to believe him, mostly because the story was so outrageous, but the truth was that I had never been that trusting of Jake, though not for any particular reason; there's just that feeling you get around some people, an uneasy twinge, like everything that comes out of their mouth falls just short of the truth.

All the same, I couldn't really explain this to Arlo, who was still staring down at me like maybe he wanted to punch me, and so finally I said, "I guess you're right. Jake probably wouldn't make that up. It's just so weird is all, you know? It's freaky-deeky, man." I forced a laugh, hoping this might ease some of the tension.

But Arlo's expression didn't change. "He didn't make it up," he said as though he hadn't even heard me. "It's totally for real."

***

There was this birthday sleepover that Mrs. Furman had tried to throw together two years earlier when me and Arlo had first started hanging out. She'd invited eight boys from our school, including me. I had accepted the invitation not knowing that everybody else had already declined, claiming that they were sick or were going out of town, and so when I heard this I had begged my mother, who had yet to find out about Jake and the whole prison thing, not to make me go. You can't have a party with just one person, I told her, and so what was the point? But she just said that me being the only one to show up would prove what a good friend I was, because imagine how I would feel if nobody showed up to my party. I told her I didn't care about proving what a good friend I was, and she said too bad, she'd already RSVP'd.

First of all, me and Arlo couldn't even watch TV, at least not for the first few hours, because Mr. Furman was watching a baseball game, so instead we just sat around and played *Risk* in Arlo's room, which was decorated with magazine cut-outs of athletes whose names he didn't know. I had to keep explaining the rules over and over to him, why all the little plastic soldiers were a different color and how each one was supposed to represent a certain number of troops. For dinner, we had tacos, one of Arlo's favorites, which were actually pretty decent, except for the shells, which I guess Mrs. Furman forgot to heat up in the microwave and so it was about like trying to crunch down on balsa wood. We all sat at the round wooden table in the corner of the kitchen, slurping up loose gobs of meat and cheese and washing them down with off-brand soda, even Jake, who was hunched over his plate like he'd just been woken from a deep sleep. He had a freshly-shaven head shaped like a bullet, and a wolf tattoo on his right forearm that you actually had to get pretty close to in order to see what it was. After dinner Mrs. Furman brought out an ice cream cake with a picture of Wolverine on top, and we all sang "Happy Birthday" and watched Arlo try to blow out the stupid trick candles, haha, except that he just ended up spraying spittle all over the cake, and so finally Mrs. Furman just picked the candles off and let Arlo's dad go ahead and cut the thing. When we'd finished, Jake burped loudly and then stood up and stretched and announced that he had to get ready to go out for the night. He gave Arlo a high-five and said "Happy birthday, dude," and then headed back out to his place above the garage. Arlo watched him leave with a look on his face like he was in love or something and then turned to me and said, "Let's go in the garage and play with the punching bag." Mr. Furman put the cake back in its box and shoved it in the freezer and then plodded back out into the TV room.

Around nine-thirty I went into the hallway bathroom and

started making these gagging sounds like I was puking, loud enough so that everybody out in the other room could hear. I thought about all the other kids who had lied their way out of the sleepover. It didn't seem right that I had to be here by myself while they got to stay home and watch TV, not playing *Risk* and not eating drippy tacos. I coughed until my face was appropriately flushed and then patted my cheeks with water from the sink and stumbled out into the TV room, clutching my belly. Mrs. Furman put her hand on my forehead and said, "My God, Kevin! Are you sick, babe?"

"I threw up."

"Should I call your mother?"

"Maybe. I don't know. I mean, I want to stay."

"I should probably call her."

Since Jake was preparing to drive over to his girlfriend's house at this time, Mrs. Furman and my mom made arrangements for him to drop me off at my house on his way into town (I had a feeling that my mom knew what I was up to, because otherwise she probably would have insisted on picking me up herself). I went into Arlo's room to gather up my things. Out in the TV room, I could hear Jake and his parents arguing about the plan. This was customary; the Furmans couldn't do anything without fighting about it first. Jake said that it would make him late, having to drop me off and everything, because he was supposed to be over at his girlfriend's place, like, right now, and anyway they hadn't asked him if he was okay with it, which was pretty goddamn inconsiderate. Mr. Furman said for Jake to stop being such a prick, that I only lived one street over for Christ's sake, and that he didn't want me getting everybody in the whole house sick. Jake said, what about me, what if he gets me sick, and Mr. Furman said: I think you'll live, son.

Arlo stood by the bedroom door with his hands in his pockets, watching me roll up my sleeping bag. "Sucks that you're sick," he said quietly.

"Yeah, dude," I replied, still clutching my belly, just to drive the point home. "Wish I didn't have to go. Like, seriously."

We walked out to the driveway where Jake was waiting for me in his dusty blue Mustang. I told Arlo I was really sorry to have to leave like this and that as soon as I felt better I would call him and we would totally play Army Commandos.

"Thanks for driving me," I said to Jake as I settled into the passenger seat with my bag in my lap. "It's just, my stomach. Man."

Without looking at me, he jerked the car out of the driveway, swinging wildly into the street, an expert maneuver.

"Don't puke," he said.

I laughed a little. "I won't. I just don't know what's wrong with me, you know? It's probably, like, a virus or something."

"A lot of that going around, I hear." His voice was drenched in that low, watery, southern business.

"Yeah. Sucks, too. I really wanted to stay over."

He chuckled like he knew something I didn't, and then he pulled a crooked cigarette out of his shirt pocket. "Yeah," he said, reaching for the lighter in the console, "that's what the other kids said, too."

Looking at him in the smoky darkness of the car, I realized that he was talking about the other boys that Arlo had invited to the party, and that he could tell I was faking, too. I knew I was supposed to feel bad about this, and I guess I did a little, but more than anything it just made me angry. Jake the Jailbird. Who was he to give me a hard time about running out on Arlo? At least I had shown up for the stupid party, which was more than you could say for all the other boys.

Besides, it wasn't like he was hanging around the house, either. In fact, the way I saw it, he had more of an obligation to Arlo than I did because they were brothers. I was pretty sure that Arlo would have agreed with this.

***

We were crouched on the fallen oak tree one afternoon looking down at Gina. It had become an after-school ritual; the bus would drop me off and I would run inside and toss my bag onto the kitchen counter and then scramble up the muddy slope of the ridge to meet up with Arlo. He was squatting down in the branches, looking through the binoculars. Out of nowhere, he turned to me and said in this weird raspy voice: "Man, I'd like to break off a piece of that."

I burst out laughing. I couldn't help it. Clearly, this was something he'd picked up from Jake. I could even picture him rehearsing it in his smelly little bedroom, repeating it over and over to himself until he'd gotten it perfect.

Arlo looked at me and smiled nervously. His doughy cheeks glowed red. "What?" he said. "I totally would."

"Yeah? What piece are you gonna break off, Arlo?" I was leaning against a large branch, trying to get my laughter under control.

"Her titties, man. They're so perfect."

Now I was laughing so hard that I had to wrap my arms around the branch to keep from falling off of the tree. This wasn't Arlo talking. It was like he was acting out some role, a poorly-crafted caricature of his brother.

Gina must have heard me then because I glanced down just in time to see her set her copy of *Marie Claire* down in her lap and look up in our direction, using her hand as a visor.

"Crap!" I whispered, swatting Arlo on the shoulder, and we leapt down from the tree and tumbled clumsily onto the cold wet ground.

Later, as we were heading back toward the playground, I asked him if he'd ever actually seen a pair of titties.

"Yeah, I've seen some," he said, a little reluctantly. He was walking a few feet behind me, kicking up pine cones and small piles of dead leaves.

"Really? When?"

"I can't remember."

I turned and gave him a look. He pretended not to notice.

"You know what?" I said after a few moments. "I bet if we went out there on Saturday night, we'd get to see Gina's titties."

"Yeah, I bet."

"Like, we'd probably see about a hundred titties. You know, at the party?"

"Yeah, and butts, too!"

"Yep. Butts, too."

He giggled loudly.

I had wanted this to sound like something I had come up with on the spot, but really I had been thinking about it ever since

Arlo had given me the background info on the Courtiers. The only reason I hadn't brought it up sooner was because I needed to be certain that he wouldn't go off and blab about it to his parents or Jake or whoever. And while I knew that it would have been easier for me to just go by myself, I figured that after all the surveillance work we'd done together, it was only fair to bring him along. And anyway, he was the one with the binoculars.

As we walked, I kept thinking back to when we'd found the panties lying on the ground at the back of the playground, how we had laughed over them for a good five minutes or so before finally dropping them back where we'd found them and then hurrying off into the woods with our guns. Only, now I couldn't figure out what it was that we had found so amusing. Really, it was kind of depressing in a way, seeing them lying there in the dark pungent mud like a trampled love note. They had seemed so intensely private, something that belonged in a drawer in somebody's sweet-smelling bedroom, hidden away from the world. Nights I would lay awake in bed and I would try to imagine the body that had once worn them. I could see her there on the moonlit playground, stepping daintily out of them into the crisp night air, grinning to herself. Yes, there she was, laying on her back on the rusty merry-go-round with her hair fanned out behind her, or bent forward on the cool metal slide, her smooth, round rear end angled up into the air, a gift for some nameless figure hovering just out of view of my imagination.

But I didn't touch myself or anything if that's what you're thinking. Not that the idea hadn't occurred to me or because I didn't know how. I just wasn't there yet, emotionally I mean. I'd seen the *Puberty and You!* video that they'd shown to all the fifth-grade boys at my school, where they'd assured us that the changes taking place to our bodies and all of our strange new urges were perfectly natural, but I still thought of masturbation as unhealthy and a little sad, a last resort for desperate people.

***

On Saturday night around eight, I headed over to the playground to meet up with Arlo. I'd told my mom that we were going to play Capture the Flag with Mark and Brice, two boys from Arlo's neighborhood. These were some of the kids that Mrs. Furman had invited to the sleepover years earlier, and the truth was they probably wouldn't have played with us if we'd paid them. It was the middle of October and the air had started getting colder and smelled a little like burning leaves. I once heard someone say that every season has a distinct smell to it, but fall is the only one I've ever noticed, when everything dries up and turns grey and crumbly.

I found Arlo hunched over in one of the swings, pushing himself idly from side to side. The binoculars were lying on the ground next to his feet, along with his paintball gun.

"Why'd you bring that?" I said, pointing to the gun.

"I thought maybe we could play some afterwards."

"It's too dark out."

He glanced down at the gun. "Yeah, I know."

"So then, how are we going to play?"

"I don't know. It wasn't that dark when I left the house." He leaned back in the swing, gripping the chains with his sausagey fingers, and looked out toward the woods on the far side of the playground. I could tell that I'd embarrassed him a little, making such a big deal about the gun. Poor Arlo. Sometimes you really felt bad for the guy. It wasn't his fault he was so big and dumb and helpless. That's just how nature works: someone always gets the short end of the stick. Most of the time, he seemed blissfully unaware of his circumstances, like an animal with some gruesome deformity. But then there were those moments of insight, like right now, when his eyes would glaze over with cruel understanding and you knew exactly what he was thinking: that he was the lowest common denominator, a kid with bad glands and a messed-up brain.

We crossed the playground and jumped the back fence and started up the hill into the woods. Arlo bumbled along behind me as usual, toting his gun and the binoculars in either hand. In another life he would have made an excellent house pet. I asked him if he was planning to dress up for Halloween.

"I'm going as Captain Jack Sparrow," he said eagerly. "There's this costume at ValuMart that me and Mom saw, and she said we could get it when Dad gets his next check. It's got, like, a wig and some makeup and a hat and stuff."

"Wow, neat."

"What's your costume?"

"I don't think I'm dressing up this year."

I glanced over my shoulder at him. He looked like he was going over some complex math equation in his head, his fat lips hanging open in a confused frown, his brow drooping down over his eyes.

"Why not?" he said.

I sighed. "I kind of feel like I'm too old maybe."

"Too old!" he laughed, a loud throaty clucking noise. "That's dumb. Like, really. You're younger than me."

"I know that." Arlo was actually a year and two months older than me.

"So then, am I too old, too?" he said.

"I don't know. I guess not. You can dress up if you want."

I could hear him panting behind me as we followed the beams of our flashlights over the slick, root-laden hills toward the Courtiers' house, through the tangles of saplings and low-hanging limbs, and I could tell that he was thinking it over, this Halloween business. After some time he said, "Hey, you know what? Maybe you could go as the other guy from the movie, Captain Jack Sparrow's friend."

"I think his name was Will," I said.

"Right. You could be him. We could go together."

We came upon the long wooden fence that ran behind the pristine cookie-cutter houses on Dexter Road. I could hear voices coming from the Courtiers' back yard, and I could see thin curls of cigarette smoke rising up over the fence. About six feet of rocky earth separated it from the point at which the ground began its steep upward slope. We turned off our flashlights and, using the coppery glow of the houses' patio lights to guide us, scrambled up the ridge to the oak tree.

Once we had positioned ourselves in the tree, I told Arlo to give me the binoculars. He was sitting on the lower end of the trunk.

"I get first look," he said stubbornly. "They're my binoculars anyway. I brought them."

"Yeah, but I'm higher up than you. I have a better view, see? I've got to take the first look to make sure the coast is clear."

I didn't really know what this was supposed to mean, but it seemed to satisfy him all the same. He nodded and then handed the binoculars up to me. I fumbled with the focus until I could make out the figures standing around the Courtiers' back yard. There were five of them, four men and one woman, all dressed in the kind of cheap white bathrobes you get at hotels, and all of them puffing away on cigarettes. I didn't see Gina or Steadman. I looked up toward the glass doors. The large blinds were drawn but had been turned open enough—unintentionally, I assumed—for me to see that the room was full of people standing around talking, holding bottles of beer and glasses of what I presumed to be liquor, just like you'd expect at any normal party, except that only a few of them were fully dressed. The rest were either wearing underwear or, in most cases, nothing at all.

"You see anything?" said Arlo. "What are they doing?"

"Don't know yet. Give me a minute."

Again, I adjusted the focus to see further back in the room. I centered in on several bodies that, still largely obscured by the blinds, appeared to be moving together on one of the loveseats in a rhythmic fashion that I could only presume was sex, S-E-X, that whole wicked affair, and suddenly it hit me that I was witnessing something monumental here, something that would undoubtedly kill off a part of me, but I'll tell you what's weird was that I actually wanted it to.

I sat there, nestled in the damp branches of the dead tree, watching the twisted little scene below and feeling like I'd slipped beneath the tender outer casing of reality into some bizarre new dimension, until after a few minutes Arlo reached up and tapped my ankle and said, "Okay, my turn."

I climbed down to the lower part of the tree where he was sitting and let him scrabble his way up to get a look inside the house.

"Look through the blinds on the back door," I said, handing him the binoculars.

Shifting his position a little—it was a tight fit for him there in the branches—he peered through them down at the party. His jaw dropped. "No way!"

"I know, right?"

"Dude! They're all, like, naked!"

While Arlo was watching the party, I took a seat on the tree trunk and went over in my head what I had seen. I had never actually seen naked adults before, except for Joe, and my mom once on accident. I felt as though something had just happened to me, that I was different in some way, though I couldn't say exactly how. And as I listened to Arlo's phlegmy cackling, I found myself once again thinking about the panties back on the playground, and about the girl who had abandoned them there. I tried to imagine where she was right then, if she was with anybody and if they were doing what I thought they might be doing. Did she wonder whatever happened to her underwear? Did she ever think back to that night on the playground, and was it a memory that made her smile the way she did in my head, or did it make her feel ashamed?

After a while I climbed up and situated myself next to Arlo, who was still peering through the binoculars, his mouth hanging open and the tip of his tongue resting on his bottom lip. "Let me look again," I said.

"Hang on a sec."

"Come on, it's my turn."

He handed me the binoculars and I looked through the kitchen window this time. I could see a small cluster of folks chatting with a kind of clumsy excitement that I figured had to do with the booze. Arlo climbed back down to the lower part of the tree. "No way," he continued chanting to himself. "Seriously, no way."

"Dude, be quiet."

"That was like—oh my god! Look at all the guys with boners! You see them, Kev? That was so hilarious."

"Shut up," I hissed, mostly because he was starting to get loud, which was something he did when he got excited and obviously we didn't want any of the folks in the back yard to hear us, but also because I had spotted something in the Courtiers' kitchen: a bald head, pale and pointy, a recognizable shape. I kept the binoculars focused on it for a few seconds until it reared back to laugh at something, and I saw that it was Jake. He was shirtless, and while I couldn't see anything below his navel, it was a safe bet that he was completely naked.

A cold breeze came through the woods, blowing thick droplets of rainwater out of the trees and down onto us.

"Jake's in there," I said, still peering down on the party.

All at once, Arlo stopped laughing. "What?" he said in a small voice.

I handed him the binoculars. "In the kitchen. Look"

He took them and pressed them to his face. I watched him as he focused in on Jake standing there by the sink, sipping a bottle of beer and talking to someone, and I saw the way that his mouth went slack and the corners of his eyes started to sag like he might cry, and it occurred to me that maybe I shouldn't have brought him out here after all.

"That's Jake," he murmured, as though saying it out loud might make it untrue, and for a moment I was certain that he really would cry. Then he dropped the binoculars into his lap and looked down on the house, like he was trying to remember something important, and that was how he stayed for some time, not saying anything, just crouching there in the thick, wet branches, and it was kind of unnerving really, like one of those moments of sad clarity he'd have from time to time, only this time there was something else there too, something a bit more severe, it seemed. It didn't occur to me then that Arlo might have felt betrayed by his brother for participating in an activity that we had been conditioned to think of as slightly shameful, maybe even a little dangerous. How could I have known that then? Half the time you couldn't tell what was going through Arlo's head.

Either way, something had him worked up and I didn't like the way he was staring down at the house, all serious and quiet and focused, like a lion stalking a pack of gazelle.

"Hey, Arlo?" I said after a while.

"Hey," he replied distantly. "Yeah?"

"I'm getting kind of cold. You want to go home?"

Clearing his throat, he lifted the binoculars back up to his face.

"Hand me my gun down there, will you Kev?"

"What, the paintball gun?"

"Yeah. Can you climb down there and get it for me?"

A few more folks stepped out into the back yard below to smoke. Somewhere behind us in the trees, an owl started hooting.

"Look, don't worry about Jake, okay?" I said. "It's not a big deal. Seriously. Who cares, right?"

But he wasn't listening anymore. He wrangled his way down from the tree, grunting as he hit the ground, and then grabbed the gun, which was leaning against the lower end of the trunk. Once he'd wrestled his way back up onto the tree and into the cage of branches, he dropped a handful of balls into the chamber and then took aim, and all I could think was that he had gone completely insane and that it was somehow my fault.

With his free hand, he made one last adjustment to the scope and then gently wrapped his finger around the trigger. I reached out for his arm, but he was too far away and I had to steady myself on the slick trunk to keep from slipping off. I started to shout at him to stop, but all I could get out was *Arlo!*

He fired, three rapid shots. The airy bursts rang out through the trees like loud sneezes, followed immediately by the thwacking sound of the paintballs splattering across the Courtiers' kitchen window, and I could see the robed figures in the yard below whip around at the sound. Crawling on my hands and knees along the fallen oak, I snatched the binoculars out of Arlo's lap and looked down just as he opened fire on the folks in the back yard. They jumped and made these little yipping noises as the paintballs hit, leaving brilliant red splotches on their robes, and then they all dropped their cigarettes and scurried into the house, clutching their heads protectively like civilians in a warzone. Through the blinds on the back door I could see the frantic flashing of legs and hair and hands, everybody rushing around to put their clothes back on.

Then the back door flew open with a cracking sound and Steadman burst out onto the patio, followed by Jake, both of them wearing white robes, and Steadman yelled something about calling the cops and how he had a handgun in his dresser drawer. Jake brushed past him out into the yard, his robe hanging open enough to reveal most of his scrawny upper body, and he spread his arms as though waiting for a fight and hollered out into the trees that if it was Arlo was up there, he was going to beat his fat fucking ass when he got home.

By that point, however, we were already on the ground dashing through the dark woods, back down the muddy leaf-covered ridge toward the school.

***

Back on the playground, we sunk down into the swings and tried to catch our breath. My legs were throbbing, and my lungs felt like they were filled with gravel. Arlo was heaving pretty hard; I was a little worried he might pass out. We didn't say anything right away, just stared out over the wet grass at the cluster of pines near the back fence. We knew what went on over there, we'd seen the evidence.

I still didn't quite understand why Arlo was so upset, and I don't think he did either, although I was starting to think maybe it wasn't just Jake, but the entire scene: all those bodies, all that skin. Ordinary folks have a hard enough time handling that kind of thing—just look at what had happened to the Courtiers back at their old place. But for someone like Arlo, who wasn't wired right to begin with and who understood sex in terms of moms and dads and making babies, I figured it was probably enough to fry a couple of fuses.

When I was finally able to breathe again, I looked over at him and said, "You cool?" This was what we said whenever one of us got a little too roughed-up playing Army Commandos—*You cool?* We'd heard it in a movie somewhere.

He leaned over and spit a thick white gob onto the worn patch of earth between his feet, and then nodded. "I think I got us in trouble."

"Maybe," I said quietly. A few moments later I was certain of this because I heard the distant cry of police sirens on the opposite side of the ridge, no doubt headed toward the Courtiers' house and then, most likely, to mine and Arlo's.

"Oh man," I muttered.

Without looking up, Arlo said, "Do you think they'll put us in jail?"

"We're too young, I think."

"There's a jail for kids, too."

"Yeah, I know."

"I really think I got us in trouble."

"We'll be okay."

"Are you mad?"

"No."

And really I wasn't, though I knew I had every right to be. In a way, I was actually a little afraid of him right then. It was like he had turned into a completely different person up there on the ridge. He wasn't even reacting to the sound of the sirens. Normally, he'd be on his feet, pissing himself with fear, looking to me to fix everything. Instead, he just sat there in the swing with his hands at his sides, gazing down at his mud-covered shoes. He seemed older somehow. I remembered how the previous year, during Fire Safety Week, some beefy guy from the fire department had come to our class and given us a lesson in first aid, during which he'd explained to us how to treat somebody who had gone into shock. *Sometimes they'll act like nothing is wrong at all,* he'd told us. *They might even get up and start walking around. Other times, though, they might just shut down completely.* That was sort of how Arlo seemed, like he was in shock.

The wind picked up then, jingling the chains of the empty swings. A few feet away, the merry-go-round groaned on its rusty axis. "I should probably go home," I said

Arlo nodded, his head still hanging there between the big balls of his shoulders. "Me too."

But neither of us stood up. Instead, what we did then was we started pushing ourselves back and forth in the swings, pumping our legs for altitude and then straightening out our bodies on the descent. Within a few moments I was flying, and I could hear Arlo grunting as he struggled to match my height. The metal frame of the swing set shuddered with each sweep of our bodies, and the cold wind snapped at our sleeves and pulled tears from the corners of our eyes.

Inflation

Rob told me he had an inflation fetish. I wasn't entirely sure how the subject had come about, but it seemed to be something he needed to get off his chest. We were sitting around my bedroom one night toward the end of the summer, sharing a bottle of red wine I'd picked up at a convenience store. He and I had been together for just over a month at this point. I was twenty-two. I had never heard of such a thing—an inflation fetish—but I didn't want to put him on the defensive, so I asked him to explain.

"It's pretty much how it sounds," he said. "I like things that inflate. Not really sure why. Some weird Freudian thing, I guess. It just turns me on. Like, a lot."

"Like balloons and stuff? That turns you on?"

"No, no. Well, not exactly. I think of breasts mostly, and I think of them expanding, like balloons, and, I don't know, it excites me."

This actually made a lot of sense. Rob was a breast guy. His idea of foreplay involved spending long periods of time kneading and prodding my tits in a way that reminded me, strangely, of one

of those laboratory chimps you see on the Discovery Channel —
more investigative than sexual. When he was done with this, he
would go at my nipples like a hungry infant, sucking until they
throbbed and had turned the color of eggplant. It was hard to say if
he got off on this or not, or rather why, but for me the whole thing
was rather tiresome. Of course, that's one thing I've learned about
sex: so much of it is very unsexy.

"What's sexual about it?" I said.

"Nothing really. But that's just how a fetish works, you know?
It's some everyday thing—shoes or whatever—that just gets you
horny."

"I see," I nodded thoughtfully and took a long look at Rob.
He was tall and lean with the incidental good looks of a cowboy:
hard lines, fair skin, and a scattering of freckles beneath his glassy
green eyes. We were still in that introductory phase of the relationship, where imperfections become a currency of trust, and by this
measure I was flattered at his willingness to engage in such a risky
transaction. But an inflation fetish? I mean, how do you respond
to that?

Frowning, he looked at the floor. "You think I'm sick."

"No, I don't."

"You do. I can tell. You're, like, freaked out."

"I'm not. I'm…intrigued."

"Seriously?"

"Seriously."

I pulled him close to me and kissed the stubbly ridge of his
jaw. He ran his thumb over my breast and smiled bashfully, a diz-
zying combination of dimples and teeth.

††

I had graduated from college earlier that year and was now
living in my mother's small house in the wooded hills outside of
Charlottesville. Four nights a week I waited tables at a downtown
bistro called Lily's. The other three nights I spent wondering, with
a considerable degree of panic, what exactly was supposed to happen next. For awhile now, I had been battling that sense of temporal stasis that usually accompanies the completion of some vital

life phase, when you realize that the obstacle you have just over-come was only standing in the way of more obstacles.

A lot of this had to do with my mother who, for several months, had been undergoing radiation treatments for a small star-shaped mass in her brain—an astrocytoma, the doctor had called it. Several days a week she would go to the hospital where they would strap her head into a vice and shoot lasers at her skull. It was there in the oncology ward that she met Ralph, a retired high school physics teacher who had been diagnosed with some kind of bone cancer. He was a tall, stately fellow with sleek silver hair and the not-so-endearing habit of conjuring quarters from behind your ears and then explaining in great detail how the trick was performed. It was the first relationship my mother had been in since my father had moved to California six years prior, and it delighted me to see the faint touch of color that would creep across her cheeks at the sound of Ralph's name.

There was one night in early fall when she called me in to the kitchen to tell me that she was moving in with him. "He's not do-ing too well on his own," she explained. "He falls down a lot and he has trouble getting back and forth from the hospital. I'm leaving you in charge."

"In charge of what?"

"Of the house, of course."

I squinted at her. "I don't want to be in charge."

"It'll be fine, Paige," she said with a note of irritation in her voice. "It's not a big deal. Just try to keep it in one piece for me."

Mom accepted her new role as Ralph's caretaker gladly, pre-paring his meals and bathing him and managing his medications, which were dispensed by the dozens. The fact of her own illness, and the subsequent radiation treatments, never seemed to bother her.

††

Rob, twenty-six at this time, was a delivery truck driver for a local produce company. We met at Lily's, which was one of the restaurants on his route. Of course, if you asked him what he did for a living, he would not readily admit to this. Instead, he would tell you that he was one of the guitarists for the band Money Shot. Most nights after their rehearsals you could find the five of them at my place, convening around a few cases of beer and a suspiciously large bag of marijuana. A good rehearsal always left them chatty and introspective, and they would fall into these weighty dialogues about the nature of stardom, the correlation between record sales and an untimely death. Once they were sufficiently trashed, they would all sit around the living room with acoustic guitars and homemade hand drums, all bleary-eyed and listless, cranking out tunes like "Hey Jude" and "Tuesday's Gone." It was something to see, really, the way they would hover over their instruments with the ritualistic air of monks, their greasy hair clinging to their foreheads, their eyes shut in looks of severe pain as they mouthed each word lovingly, until after a few hours when their voices would begin to grow thin and to crack and the songs would devolve into these sloppy drunken dirges. By three AM the charm was usually gone. In the mornings it was not uncommon for me to find them in the living room, sprawled out on the couches or on the floor, their nicotine-yellowed fingers still wrapped around the necks of their guitars.

††

Because of the tumor's location in Mom's brain—somewhere near the temporal lobe—the doctors had decided that surgery was too much of a risk. She relied solely upon the radiation treatments, which had inhibited the tumor's growth up to this point, but had done nothing to reduce its size. And yet, to look at her, you wouldn't suspect that this was a woman who'd been given a year at the most to live. She still had all of her hair, and her skin hadn't yet taken on that sickly pinkish-grey complexion I associated with most of the other folks in the oncology ward who were as far along in their treatments as she was. In fact, the only evidence of her condition was a mild slurring of her speech, and even this she was able to to pass off as a deep southern accent.

On Monday mornings she would come by the house before her treatments to pick up her mail. I did my best on these days to make the place look presentable. I would wake up early and scrub dishes and vacuum rugs and spray air freshener in every room. After rousing the band, I would hand one of them a garbage bag full of empty bottles and send them home. This included Rob. It didn't feel right having him there while my mother was visiting, even though she had repeatedly expressed her fondness for him, and how comforting it was for her to know that there was someone in the house to look after me.

After she had sifted through the pile of envelopes, Mom and I would sit at the kitchen table sipping weak coffee, and she would fill me in on Ralph's condition. "His appetite is a little better. Last night he ate an entire enchilada. 'Don't overdo it,' I said. He's always trying to impress me. He hates it when I worry."

††

Money Shot was the kind of band you had to see live to appreciate, which is to say that it didn't hurt to be a little drunk. For me there was a sort of adolescent pride in being associated with the band, which might have been the only thing that enabled me to tolerate their fans, these teenage pinup-types, all hips and midriffs and impossible chests. It wasn't that I considered myself unattractive—I had been blessed with my mother's demure Eastern European features, her soft shadowy eyes and honey-colored complexion—but around these girls it was impossible not to feel like a mutant, so it was gratifying to know that I had something over them, something they wanted and couldn't have. I would sit near the back of the venue, away from the crowd, and I would watch eagerly as the five young men took the stage with the postured swagger of young warriors returning home from a hunt. There was always a few minutes of tuning before they launched into some anthem of corporate impiety, which would invariably drive the crowd into an orgiastic tangle of limbs and hair.

One night, toward the end of the show, a girl from the crowd approached me. I was seated at a small table near the bar, nursing a watered-down mojito. She was tall and dangerously slim, dressed in leather pants and a man's sleeveless t-shirt. One look and it was clear that she was in deep orbit. Her eyes, red and dilated, rolled wildly in their sockets. The acetone smell of vodka seemed to be drifting from her pores, and as I watched her struggle to light a cigarette, I was almost certain that she would burst into flames.

"Would you look at them?" she said, motioning toward the stage. Her voice was sort of dreamy and disconnected, like someone talking in her sleep. "What is it about musicians that makes them so goddamn fuckable?"

I was struck by the unintended poignancy of this question. There was something, wasn't there? A glow, an ache, something. I looked toward the stage where Rob was wielding his guitar like a piece of artillery, his black hair fringed by the smoky lights. He was wearing a ratty white undershirt that emphasized the sleek, delicious contours of his chest and stomach. After a moment, I looked back at the girl, with her runny makeup and her tussled hair. There was a slow, calculated quality to her movements, as though she were underwater. I pointed at her cigarette. "I think you lit the wrong end."

She made a sound that was half-laughing, half-belching. Her head lolled. "Fuckin' for real!"

††

As Ralph's condition worsened, Mom's Monday morning visits grew increasingly shorter. She would stride into the house looking evermore weary and thin, and she would spend a few minutes sorting through the small pile of mail before muttering something about painkillers before rushing off again. Our conversations were reduced to curt little sentence fragments: *Job okay? Hi to Rob.*

In retaliation, I stopped cleaning the house. I've never been the messy type—even in college, I dusted my apartment regularly and organized the items in my fridge according to size and expiration date—and so this actually required much more effort than I had anticipated. Within a week or so, the stove and countertops were completely covered with empty bottles. In every room were stacks of dirty dishes encrusted with the remnants of unidentifiable foods. I let Rob and the others smoke inside; they used coffee mugs and plastic cups as ashtrays. If they had stayed over the night before, I left them sleeping on whatever piece of furniture they had procured. It wasn't long before the house had taken on the thick, meaty reek of a high school cafeteria.

"What the hell have you been doing in here, Paige?" Mom said one morning. "It smells awful."

I was seated at the kitchen table, dabbing at a bowl of instant oatmeal. "The guys were over pretty late," I replied, not looking up.

She sighed offhandedly. "Really, I don't know how you can live like this. I certainly couldn't."

"I'm young. It's what we do."

I peered up her, awaiting a reprimand, hoping for one actually. What was I? Just a guest in her home, was all. I wanted her to scold me for my terrible housekeeping skills, for the four smelly men snoring in the living room, for the one currently sleeping in my childhood bed. Instead, she simply shrugged and mumbled something about Ralph and a PET scan and then headed for the door. Her scent lingered, a mixture of skin cream and chemicals. I continued poking at my oatmeal. From down the hall I heard Rob get up and use the bathroom and then stumble back into the bedroom.

††

Rob told me about an inflatable suit he'd seen on the internet, a sort of latex bubble designed for fetishists of his variety. It was the first time in several weeks that he'd mentioned the inflation thing, and I had sort of been hoping he had let it go. He tried to pass it off as small talk, but he couldn't disguise the eager undertone of his voice.

"Are you going to buy it?" I said. It was early morning and we were lying in bed after a clumsy drunken romp that I'm not sure even qualified as sex. The oily stench of our bodies hung heavy around us.

"I don't know. Would you wear it?"

"I don't know," I replied, scowling a little. "Is that all I have do? Just put it on?"

"Yeah, pretty much."

"Are we supposed to fuck or what?"

"No, but that's, you know—that's not really the point."

Despite my growing suspicions of Rob's sexual predilections, I was strangely fascinated by this idea. An inflatable suit. I thought of that girl from *Willy Wonka and the Chocolate Factory*, the one who had turned into a giant blueberry, and I imagined myself as such, this enormous human sphere being rolled back forth from person to person, limbless, obediently traveling in whichever direction I was pushed.

A few weeks later the suit arrived in the mail and Rob brought it over to my house. "You're so cool for doing this," he said as he carried the box inside. He'd instructed the band to take the night off, a gesture that seemed to have imbued him with an absurd sense of gallantry. I followed him into my bedroom where he shoved all the furniture up against the far wall and then, with an idiotic grin, pulled the suit out of the box and held it up for me to inspect. It looked like something you might wear when handling toxic waste: the inner layer was a thin full-body leotard, and the outer layer was flesh-colored plastic that, when fully inflated, was supposed to resemble the body of a violently obese woman, complete with breasts the size of beach balls and nipples as large as fists.

After I'd stripped and managed to fight my way into the leotard, Rob attached an air compressor to a small valve on the right ankle of the suit. Slowly, the thing began to inflate, and he lay back on the bed to watch.

"Is this all I do?" I said. I was standing in the corner of the room in front of the door.

"Uh-huh."

"What are you going to do?"

Smiling maliciously, he reached for his zipper. "Just relax now."

I was either too amused or too disgusted to move. Little by little, the suit began to take on its improbable shape. The arms and legs swelled to the size of tree trunks, locking me into a rigid stance. As the pressure built up inside the plastic, I was steadily overtaken by an unnerving sense of dislocation, as though my body was shrinking away entirely, being replaced, which I suspected Rob might have enjoyed. I thought of the few feminist literature courses I had taken in college, and I wondered, somewhat shamefully, what those grave French women with their theories on phallocentrism and female objectification might have said if they could have seen me then. For some reason, it was hard not to watch the up-and-down motion of Rob's hand, or the way he kept licking his teeth.

This is really happening, I thought. *Fuckin' for real!*

"Okay, I'm not doing this," I said finally. I tried to bend over and reach for the valve, but the suit made maneuvering almost impossible.

Rob continued his stroking. "Hang on. I'm almost done."

"No, I want out of this thing now."

"But you look so hot."

"Now, Rob!"

He sat up on the bed. His erection pointed at me, an accusation. "But you said you were into this. I mean, why did I buy the suit, Paige?"

"I don't fucking know!"

Again, I tried to waddle my way around to the air compressor, but I lost my balance and toppled forward onto the floor, bouncing slightly on the ridiculous breast-balloons. The thick plastic made a squeaking sound like an injured rodent. When I came to rest, there was nearly a foot of space between me and the carpet. My hair formed a curtain around my face.

Rob leapt off the bed and switched off the compressor. "Careful!" he whined. "You'll break it!"

††

I walked into the kitchen one morning to find Rob and my mother seated next to one another at the table. This was shortly after the incident with the suit, and my bitterness toward Rob had not completely disappeared, so I was mildly appalled to see the familiar way he was leaning into her, clutching her hand on the table like they were old friends. Mom's face was red and glossy from crying, and there were several balled-up Kleenexes on the table.

I took a seat across from them and asked her what was wrong. "Ralph went into the hospital again last night," she said, straightening up in her chair a little, trying to regain some composure. "The doctors think its pretty close now, a few weeks maybe."

I laid my hand on their small mound of fingers. "Are you moving back here?"

She shook her head. "No, I just needed my address book. There's going to be a lot to take care of at his place, the family and all. I'm going to be there for a while."

Rob glanced up at me, arched his eyebrows, and then looked back at Mom.

"I want you to come back here," I said.

"Honey, I have to deal with this right now, okay?"

"Why can't you just let the doctors handle it? Why is at all up to you?"

She gripped the sides of her head. "I don't want to argue right now, Paige."

"You need someone to take care of you."

"Jesus! Don't be so dramatic." Her slurring, which had grown more evident, gave her words a lifeless, robotic quality. "Who's going to take care of me? You? Look at this place," she huffed indignantly, sweeping a hand through the air. "It's disgusting. Look at the sink. Those dishes have been there for nearly a month. You don't even know how to take care of yourself."

"I know better than Ralph does."

Mom gaped at me; her stunned silence was enough to know that I'd hit a nerve. And really, I was glad. Because it was then that I realized how much I had grown to hate Ralph. I might have even hated her too then, just a little, because I had no one else to blame for what was happening, and because, in a way, isn't dying just another way of leaving?

Rob had this look on his face like he was being mugged at gunpoint.

"Well, that's just lovely," Mom said quietly, more to herself it seemed. She gathered up the used tissues and tossed them into the trash. "Very adult of you, Paige. I'm so glad I stopped by."

She stalked toward the door, making it a point not to look at me as she passed. Moments later we heard her car backing out of the driveway. Rob and I stood there in the kitchen, speechless. I can't say I was feeling entirely guilty about what had just happened.

"What is the matter with you?" he said after a few moments. "That's your mother."

"Thank you. I'm aware of that."

"Why are you acting like this?"

"Look, this isn't your problem, okay?"

"Can't you see what she's going through?" He was standing on the opposite side of the small cedar table with his hands planted on the back of one of the wooden slatback chairs. "Her boyfriend is dying, and she has to sit there and watch it happen."

"No, she doesn't! No one twisted her arm to be there. It was her choice. She could move back here. She doesn't want to be with me."

"Oh my god! You don't get it at all!"

"I want you to leave."

"Paige, look. She's scared. She doesn't want you to see what's going to happen to her."

"I said go!"

With a bitter laugh, he headed for the door. "Fine. Great. Whatever. You've got a real bitchy side, you know that?"

"Fuck you."

"Yeah, right."

††

Money Shot was performing at a club downtown that night, but I didn't go. I spent most of the evening lying around the dark, greasy-smelling living room, watching television and feeling sorry for myself. I had this image of my mother scurrying about Ralph's hospital room, fluffing his pillows and wiping his face and pestering the nurses for test results, and I wondered how long it would be until I was in her position. Rob called around eleven, during the band's set break, just as had I presumed he would. In the background I could hear the excited warbling of the crowd and the clinking of glasses.

"Look," he said a bit peevishly, "I'm not saying I was wrong or that you weren't bitchy. But the thing is, I know what you're going through right now must be hard."

"Do you?"

"Yes. Well, not personally, but I can understand it. I'm trying to fix things here."

"Is that an apology?"

He let out an agitated sigh. "I just don't like fighting with you, okay?"

For a few moments I was silent. I thought about the argument that morning. It had occurred to me shortly after I'd kicked him out of the house that at some point—I wasn't prepared to say exactly when—I was going to be the one to end things between him and me, not necessarily because I wanted to, but because I knew that Rob never would. He was content with me, you could say, mostly because he didn't know any better. Which, to be fair, is more than you get from most people. And knowing this, I couldn't help thinking that it would have been much easier for both of us if he had just never called me again.

Over the phone I heard the sharp squeal of feedback from an amplifier and the muffled sound of someone speaking into a microphone. "Paige?" said Rob. "You there? I've got to go back on."

"I'm here. It's okay. Enjoy the show."

After I had gotten off the phone with Rob, I went to my bedroom closet where I'd stashed the suit after its single use. I pulled it out and spread it on the bed like an expensive piece of clothing, and I studied it for a few moments. What was it about the idea of this thing that had once appealed to me? It wasn't just the image of the blueberry girl from *Willy Wonka*. No, there was something else, the suggestion of growth maybe. Now I found myself once again fighting my way into the stubborn leotard, which was a bit like trying to stuff your whole body into a single stocking. Once I had made my way into the suit, I hooked up the air compressor and lay down on the floor and watched the shiny plastic unfold and take shape as the cool air slithered all around me, the pressure building up inside until finally, after a couple of minutes, my body began to rise from the floor, slowly and delicately, and I imagined myself as some priceless artifact nestled in the palm of an enormous hand, something that a person might go to great lengths to protect.

Reshma

On a Wednesday night in August, Caleb Waltz, 13, pedaled down Carter Avenue toward Reshma Mohammadian's house. He was going to deliver the mix tape he'd made for her after her brother Farhad had dropped dead out on the school track the previous week. The plan was to attach it to her window screen using the ring of duct tape he wore around his wrist so that when she opened her curtains in the morning it would be the first thing she saw. He ascended the hill at the end of Carter, standing up in order to push the pedals, and then swung right onto the shoulder of Van Meter Road, winding expertly through the mangled beer cans and the constellations of glass shards glinting in the gutter beneath the street lights. The cool wind whipped his shaggy blond hair across his eyes and stretched his t-shirt back across his scrawny frame. On his left, cars hurtled past, spewing fans of water from that afternoon's rains and trailing strong gusts of air that were liable to send you flying if you weren't prepared for them. But Caleb had made the trip out to Reshma's house many times, or, more specifically, to the woods next to her house, and so he knew now to lean into the air stream whenever a car passed, not much, an inch or two maybe, just enough to keep from toppling over into the gutter.

He'd started the rides out to Reshma's a year earlier after Nana had been diagnosed with Alzheimer's, a disease neither Caleb nor his older sister Cassie understood all that well, beyond the fact that it seemed to be steadily eating away at her brain. A couple nights a week, usually after one of Nana's and Cassie's shrill shouting matches, he would sneak out the back door to retrieve his bike, telling himself that he was just going for a ride around the neighborhood to clear his head. Inevitably though, he would find himself pedaling the mile and a half to Reshma's so he could sit in the dark woods outside her window, watching the soft orange glow from inside and contriving fantasies in which he had to go live in those woods because Nana had kicked him out of the house—as she had his eighteen-year-old sister Cassie a month earlier. And in this fantasy Reshma would find him there sleeping in a nest of dead leaves and, moved by his manly fortitude and his apparent desire to be near her—even if it meant living off of berries and caterpillars for who knows how long—she would invite him into her room, the sweet-smelling warmth of it, and they would kiss a little bit, sure, and maybe things would get kind of steamy and there'd be some touching and some muted moans, but it was always that offer for him to climb through the window that Caleb focused on more than anything: just getting in there, that was the important part. And while he knew there'd be hell to pay if anybody ever found out what he was doing out in the trees next to the Mohammadians' house—especially from Nana, whose *condition*, as the folks at church tended to refer to it in defeated whispers, had worsened steadily over the past year and had evoked in her a real a nasty streak that at times made Caleb wonder if maybe she was possessed by some evil spirit, the way she would curse at him and call him by the wrong name, as in, *"Gordon, get the fuck out there and check the fucking gate already!"*—this sense of risk only reinforced Caleb's belief that what he was doing, this *spying* if you really wanted to call it that, was, when you got down to it, actually kind of romantic.

He passed the Markleys' house, where he used to go after

school back before Nana got too sick to work anymore. Skirting the small silver puddles gleaming against the broken curb, he felt a slight pang of something that might have been sadness, though he couldn't be sure; these days, when it came to Nana, Caleb was often unsure how he was supposed to feel. He and Cassie had come to live with her six years earlier when their mother and her boyfriend Skip had gone to prison for some financial scam they'd been involved in. The details of it had never been made clear to Caleb, though he knew that it had something to do with elderly people and credit cards. Nana had been working in the gift shop in the hospital downtown back then, a job she'd held for the past twenty-five years. On Sunday mornings during services, she volunteered in the church nursery, where she could be found cooing sweetly at the squealing infants and saying things like "Oh, I think somebody made a mess, Mr. Saggy Diaper Man!" Most of her spare time she spent at home in the kitchen, scrubbing the floors and counter tops and scouring the grimy innards of the oven, activities that seemed to enliven her in a way that Caleb and Cassie found both endearing and a little sad, but now whenever Caleb thought back to those first few years, this was the image that always came to mind: Nana, wearing sweatpants and a t-shirt and a pair of yellow dish gloves, hunched over the pea-colored stovetop with a Brillo pad in her hand, swathed in the oddly comforting aroma of Comet disinfectant.

It was difficult to say precisely when she'd started getting sick. She'd always had a tendency to forget things, names and days of the week and where she had left her purse the night before—things that were easy enough for her to laugh off and chalk up to old age. "I swear I'd lose my head if it wasn't attached to me," she'd say, smiling. But it was when she started mistaking Caleb for other people—usually one of her older brothers, all of whom had been dead for more than a decade—that he and Cassie began to understand it was more than just old age.

Then there was the Saturday morning a year ago when she'd had one of her fits on the bus on her way to work and had wound up at the end of the route on the far side of town, too confused and belligerent to leave her seat. It had taken the police forty-five minutes to coax her off, after which they'd taken her to the station nearby and held her there until they were able to get a hold of Cassie. By the time she and her boyfriend Jay, with whom she'd stayed the night before, had arrived to pick her up, Nana's fit had passed, leaving her in a state of mild panic at the fact that she could not recall how or why she had ended up at a police station.

This was the incident that had ultimately led her physician to diagnose her with Alzheimer's and, consequently, to recommend her forced retirement from the gift shop. Since then she'd grown steadily thinner and weaker, spending most of her time in front of the tiny black and white television in her bedroom and tumbling through increasingly shorter states of lucidity.

Now Caleb passed the two-story stucco house with the lonely dead dogwood in the corner of the yard and the Christmas lights that blinked year-round, and then he crossed the road and jumped the curb and sped down the grassy slope into the small bowl of land where the creek cut a murky trench through the stubborn scrub. At the bottom of the hill, he leapt off his bike, moving carefully so as not to damage the plastic cassette case in his pocket, and propped the bike against a tree. Then, with small careful steps in the dark, he found the narrow spot in the creek and jumped across and scrabbled up the other side of the land-bowl. Reshma's house was at the top of the hill, a small rust-colored place overlooking the Shuford highway on the opposite side.

At the top of the hill, he came upon the chainlink fence running the length of the Mohammadians' back yard. The cuffs of his jeans, soaked from the damp cheatgrass, clung to his bare ankles. He didn't want to go right up to the window without making sure that there was nobody around inside to catch him, so he crept along in the dark hunched over, trying this best to avoid the buttery glow of the back porch flood light, until he made it to the side of the house where the fence stopped, and he darted into the woods a dozen or so yards away, where, after edging through the branches, he found the magnolia tree where he usually stationed himself, and he crawled through the wall of stiff leaves into the bare interior and then looked out, monitoring the house for any signs of activity.

It excited Caleb to think how Reshma might react when she found the tape the following morning, whether or not it would bolster her opinion of him in the way he hoped it would, so that maybe when she came back to school she would tell Laney and Hillary in homeroom not to call him "Spoonchest" anymore and not to ask him if that's where he ate his corn flakes in the morning. He liked to think back to the day she'd shown up in class in the first grade, a skinny girl with black hair and olive skin and big brown eyes that when you looked at them, *really* looked at them, made you realize that it was over, all of it—that you were a goner. That was six years ago, just a couple months after the state had transferred him and Cassie to Nana's house, and Reshma had spoken to him only once since then—last year in Social Studies, she'd leaned over the aisle one afternoon and asked him what day the midterm was on—but even now, hunkered down on the spongy floor around the magnolia tree with the flat pressure of the tape on his thigh, Caleb felt the same way he'd felt that morning six years earlier, like he was doomed somehow, and it was a good feeling, big and exhilarating.

The light was on in the room next to Reshma's, which had been Farhad's, and Caleb wondered what was going on in there at that moment. Maybe they were packing up the boy's things, his trophies and clothes and whatnot. A couple times in the past while watching Reshma's window, Caleb had seen Farhad in his room, rifling through drawers or talking to somebody on the phone, and one time he'd seen him standing naked in front of the full length mirror mounted on the closet door, twisting through a series of strange poses, sulkily examining his chest and biceps. He was tall and lean with arms that seemed just a bit too long for his lanky frame. He had been something of a local celebrity ever since he'd broken the national high school records for the eight hundred and the thousand-meter dashes at a track meet in Longview earlier that year. *The Nix Dispatch* had dedicated half the front page to an article about him, and there had been some talk about athletic scholarships, LSU or maybe Tulane, full rides all the way.

And so it was especially difficult to make sense of what had happened to him out on the track last week. Caleb had heard about it from Ricky Lucas, whose brother Randy was on the cross country team with Farhad. They'd been running laps when Farhad had stumbled and gone down hard onto the track. This happened from time to time, Ricky was careful to point out, guys falling, either from a misstep or from pure exhaustion, and so there wasn't any real concern, not until after a couple of Farhad's teammates had helped him up and back over to the bench where, upon being released, he'd collapsed onto the rough red clay and died, just like that, as though something had snatched the life right out of his body.

The school had canceled all remaining home track events for the term, and the *Dispatch* had run another article about Farhad, a full-pager this time, in which they had stated that his death was the result of a brain aneurysm, and then just a couple nights ago there had been a candlelight vigil out at the track, a few hundred people, students and parents and teachers, moping around in the tidy green grass encircled by the track with their arms around each others' shoulders, clutching candles in paper sconces and singing "Amazing Grace" and the Nix High fight song. In lieu of attending the vigil, Caleb had ridden his bike the two miles over to the school that night and sat up on the hill near the tennis courts and looked down on the event, listening to the chorus of weepy voices carry out into the dim blue night, a sound that could have been mistaken for a single voice, he considered, if you were far enough away.

Later that night, long after Nana had fallen asleep, Caleb had wandered into Cassie's room. There was something about the vigil that had evoked in him some biting need to glimpse the abandoned clutter of her life—the unmade bed, the piles of dirty clothes on the floor, the dresser drawers hanging open like awed mouths. Standing there in the middle of his sister's room, he'd felt like a tourist in the aftermath of some natural disaster, the way everything seemed to hang suspended in a single moment of panic. However, when he spotted the CD player on the far side of the room, he realized why he'd stumbled in here in the first place. He stepped gingerly over a pair of black combat boots and a pile of magazines and sat down on the brown shag rug in front of it. There was a stack of blank tapes on top of one of the speakers. Cassie had been an avid tapemaker; each season or holiday in the Waltz house was marked by some compilation that she would blast from her stereo for weeks at a time, much to Nana's annoyance. Caleb grabbed one and peeled off the shrinkwrap, then began fumbling through the plastic milk crate of CDs sitting nearby, selecting artists that he'd heard Cassie talk about, REM and the Pixies and Elvis Costello. He'd worked late into the night, listening to each album in its entirety and then selecting the songs that he thought might somehow offer Reshma a little consolation while also expressing to her the many fathoms of his sophistication.

Presently, rain water trickled down from the trees outside Reshma's room until Caleb's t-shirt and shoes were soaked. By this point it had become clear she wouldn't be coming to her window any time soon, that in all likelihood she wasn't even home, probably at a relative's or something, and so finally Caleb crept out of the woods and over to the window, where he squatted down in the grass and reached into his pocket for the tape, and that was when he noticed the figure standing in the shadows of the big oak tree in the nearby corner of the back yard. Actually, it was the glow of the man's cigarette that first caught his attention, a small orange dot in the dark, which made Caleb freeze in place, kneeling beneath the brick window ledge, praying that by some stroke of luck he had gone unnoticed. But when the man raised a hand in greeting, Caleb stood up straight and, somewhat reluctantly, returned the gesture, wondering with a distant unease what sort of punishment Nana would dole out whenever the Mohammadians, the poor, sad, grieving Mohammadians, called her to explain that her grandson had been prowling around the woods outside of their daughter's window.

The man took a few steps toward Caleb and placed his hands on the top rail of the fence, his cigarette smoldering between his fingers. "Hello," he said, and Caleb could tell from his accent—Middle Eastern; rough, but somehow elegant—that this was Reshma's father.

"Hi," said Caleb.

"What are you doing?"

Caleb took a breath and stood up, brushing the grass off his knees.

"Nothing," he said, but then immediately realized how ridiculous this sounded, so he added: "I've got this thing I was supposed to give to Reshma."

"What thing?"

"It's just, like, this tape I made her. Some songs and stuff. It's dumb." He shrugged and rocked back on his heels. When the man didn't say anything, Caleb continued: "I mean, I was supposed to give it to her. I was just going to leave it on the window here because I figured it was kind of late and I didn't want to knock on the door or whatever. That's all I was doing. I was supposed to give it to her."

The man—Mr. Mohammadian—took a long drag of his cigarette and exhaled a mouthful of bluish smoke into the air, and then coughed into his fist and said: "Come over here."

Slowly, Caleb made his way toward the fence, his legs wobbling as though his muscles were evaporating. As he approached, the shadows parted and the man's face came into view; it was long and full of hard angles and planes, like something carved out of wood, but in a hurry.

"Let me see it," the man said.

Caleb retrieved the cassette case from his pocket and handed it to Mr. Mohammadian. The man turned it over in his hand, examining the hand-written track listing and the large FOR RESHMA printed in careful blue letters on the spine, gazing absently at the thing as though it were a kind of puzzle, something that needed to be solved. Finally, he handed the tape back to Caleb, and said, "What's your name?"

"Caleb."

"How old are you?"

"Thirteen. Except I'll be fourteen in two weeks."

The man nodded deeply, an exaggerated gesture. Then, in a far away kind of voice, he said: "Do you like baseball?"

Caleb looked up into the man's eyes for the first time and was startled by the way they seemed to quaver in his puffy sockets, as though poised to burst from his head. The expression on his hard face was frighteningly similar to the look that would come over Nana whenever she went into one of her fits and started cursing and calling Caleb by the wrong names: angry and lost and sleepy all at once.

"Yeah, I do," Caleb replied.

The man took another drag off his cigarette. "I do, too. There is a league in the town that I used to play on. I was good shortstop. What is the position you play?"

"I don't really have one. Just anything, I guess."

"Would you like to play baseball?"

"Right now?"

There was that over-animated nod again. "We will toss the ball. Play some catch, yes?"

Caleb looked around at the dark yard, the dewy weeds and snarls of tree roots entangled in the bottom of the fence. He felt a kind of buzzing in his chest that threatened to turn him inside out if he didn't make a decision quick. He had played T-ball as a kid, only because that was what you did in summers when you were too young to know any better, and he and Cassie had tossed the ball around in the back yard once or twice over the years, but there was a galaxy of difference between playing catch with your sister and with some guy who played shortstop in a town league. But something in him would not let him say no to Mr. Mohammadian. How could he? Maybe it was because the man had just lost a kid and appeared to have slipped into a mild psychosis, or maybe because he had caught Caleb skulking around his daughter's window, and he had every right to call the cops. Finally he said: "I guess maybe for a few minutes. But I can't play for real long. I've got to get home in a while."

Mr. Mohammadian tapped the fence rail with his palm, rattling the rusty wire. Caleb leaned away from him a little. "We play in the front yard, okay? There's not so many trees." He swung an arm through the air, gesturing, apparently, to the large back yard. "Too many trees here, yes?"

"Okay. But I don't have a glove."

"I have an extra."

"Okay," Caleb said again, quickly adding: "But I really can't be out real late."

"No, not too late. I will go get the gloves and a ball. I will meet you in front yard, okay?"

Caleb nodded and said sure, and then Mr. Mohammadian turned and strolled across the back yard, past the rusted-over jungle gym that you could tell hadn't been played on in maybe a decade, and into the warm cone of light spreading out from the house across the overgrown grass. His stride was wide and airy, his long legs seeming to search out the ground in front of him like a pair of antennae. To anybody else he might have looked like a man happily lost in thought, but to Caleb he just looked like he was missing part of his mind.

Caleb headed around the front of the house, past Reshma's and Farhad's windows, into the long narrow front yard, which was mottled with weeds and the corpses of unidentifiable plants lining the small concrete walkway snaking up to the front step. He took the tape out of his pocket and set it and the ring of duct tape on the bottom step for the time being. Then he moved over into the driveway and looked out toward the edge of the yard where the ground dropped off suddenly toward the highway, a good six feet maybe, and he could hear the wet hiss of the cars speeding along the steamy asphalt below. During the holidays, there was this big inflatable Santa that the Mohammadians would put up in the front yard that would wave at the traffic, despite the fact that, as Cassie had pointed out to him, they didn't actually celebrate Christmas, being from Iran and all. But Caleb guessed you didn't necessarily have to be a Christian to get wrapped up in the whole Santa Claus thing. People like big inflatable things waving at them; sometimes it really was that simple.

The front door opened, and Mr. Mohammadian strode out into the yard carrying a couple of mitts, his arms swinging in an attitude of forced casualness, and Caleb smiled weakly and pretended to shake out his hands and feet. He was going to toss the ball with Reshma Mohammadian's father. They were going to play catch. How do these things happen? He wasn't sure how to answer that question or even if it could be answered, but it didn't matter now anyway because here was Mr. Mohammadian crossing the yard to where he stood in the driveway and handing one of the gloves to him and then motioning to the opposite side of the yard and saying, "I will go over there, okay?"

"Okay."

The man turned and trotted across the grass, stopping about a dozen yards short of the woods and pulling a ball out of his mitt and slapping it into the glove a few times. Then he wound up, slowly, executing this little kick move that seemed more comical than practical, and he lobbed the ball to Caleb. For a moment it was suspended in the milky gleam of the porch light, a spinning white orb of doom, and Caleb held his glove up in front of his face, keeping his eye on the ball like his coaches had always told him to do when he was a kid—this was the only piece of advice he'd retained from his t-ball days—and a moment later he felt the stiff smack of the ball in the mitt.

He looked down. There was the ball.

Well okay.

Letting out a breath, he tossed it back over to Mr. Mohammadian and then watched, smiling, as the man reached out and plucked the thing from the dark, graceful as a pirouette.

Pretty soon they had worked themselves into a comfortable rhythm, catch, throw, catch, throw, and Caleb began to feel a bit more at ease. It was a good feeling, refreshing really, throwing a ball out in the cool evening air while the cars zoomed past on the road below. There was something to it all, a sense of things coming together: he wasn't just doing this for Mr. Mohammadian anymore. He managed to snag most of the tosses, and the ones he missed were usually the result a miscalculated trajectory on the man's part or because the ball sailed too close to the bright porch light, and each time he missed, Mr. Mohammadian would call out "S'okay!" as Caleb scrambled to retrieve it.

He found himself thinking about the Big Fight a month earlier, when Cassie had left for good. She and Nana had been in the kitchen discussing the family's annual trip to Shreveport the following weekend for the Fourth of July. It was a tradition: the family from around the state would congregate at Nana's sister Jackie's house each year for the holiday weekend. Nana and Jackie and the rest of the adults would head downtown to the riverboats to play the slots and maybe see a show, while Caleb and Cassie and their younger cousins would wander down along the riverbank, watching the street performers—elderly black men with electric guitars and portable amps, teeth like the remnants of bombed-out cities— and ducking in and out of museums. Caleb was particularly fond of the antique car museum, a large glassy building that housed several dozen lavish vehicles, including an orange Duisenberg that the owner, a woman about Nana's age, would let him sit in if there were no other patrons. Then, in the evening, the family would head back to Jackie's large sprawling ranch house to grill burgers on the deck and, if the weather was right, start a bonfire. Because it was the closest thing to a vacation that Caleb and his sister had been able to take since their mother's incarceration, they looked forward to it each year.

This year, however, Cassie's boyfriend Jay had won concert tickets from a local radio station. The concert was the same night as the party. "I feel like maybe I'm a little too old for it, anyway," Cassie had said to Nana in the kitchen on the night in question. "It's nothing against Jackie or anything. I just think I've outgrown the whole thing, you know?"

"You've outgrown it?" Nana replied bitterly, and Caleb, seated on the sofa in the next room, could tell from the low, raspy sound of her voice that this was one of her bad moments coming, one of her fits, and he prayed that Cassie would pick up on this too and just drop the whole thing, but she had never been as adept at forecasting Nana's sudden mood swings.

"I don't wanna get into a big thing about it," Cassie had said with a loud sigh, and Caleb felt his muscles grow rigid and tight, an airplane passenger bracing for an emergency landing. "I'm not going to Shreveport. I'm going to the show with Jay."

From here the conversation had deescalated into one of their customary shouting matches, their voices steadily rising, rising, filling the house like a stench, until it was almost impossible to breathe.

Finally, Nana bellowed: "You'd rather be with him than your family, then you get on out of here and go be with him!" Her voice would have been fitting for a cartoon witch. "I don't want you here anymore, anyhow! You're an ungrateful bitch! Get on out of my house!" When Cassie, transfixed by the ferocity in the woman's voice, didn't move, Nana had screeched: *Get the fuck on out!*"

Without another word, Cassie had turned and marched down the hall to her room, wiping tears and snot from her face, and began stuffing clothes in a duffel bag, a couple of shirts and some underwear and a pair of jeans. Caleb had followed her and then stood in her doorway trying to calm her. She had to have known that this wasn't actually Nana talking, that it was all part of her condition. "Her brain is all messed up," he'd said timidly, standing there with his hands shoved deep in his pockets—a nervous habit—trying hard to keep from crying. "Seriously, you don't have to leave, Cass. She's sick, that's all." But Cassie had just shaken her head and reached down and brushed the hair out of his eyes and said softly: "There's sickness, and then there's sickness." She pointed down the hall to the kitchen where Nana was still babbling to no one in particular. "But that woman is a fucking nightmare, and I'm just over it." It was something she said whenever she was frustrated—*I'm over it*—although this time it seemed to carry an unusual weight. Caleb trailed her to the front door and then stood out on the step and watched hopelessly as her car squealed out of the driveway and took off down the road, toward Jay's apartment, where she'd been staying ever since. Moments later he heard Nana's psychotic voice rumble up from the back of the house: *Where's Michael? Where's the goddamn saddle?*

He was remembering this as he held his glove out to snag one of Mr. Mohammadian's lazy lobs, but he lost it in the porch light again and the ball struck the tip of the glove and, glancing left, bounced toward the edge of the yard. He scrambled after it, tripping lamely and falling to his knees and elbows in the cold wet grass just as the ball disappeared over the lip of the steep slope, rolling down into road. "Let it go, it's okay," said Mr. Mohammadian, taking a couple steps toward him, but Caleb was so alight with panic at the thought of spoiling the game that the words did not even register. He'd lost the man's ball! There it was, rolling across the busy highway below and coming to rest in the gutter on the other side. Struggling up out of the grass, he hobbled over to the edge of the slope, and again Mr. Mohammadian said, "Just let it go," a bit louder this time, but Caleb ignored him and instead squatted down on the edge of the slope, preparing to hoist himself down into the small trough of land next to the shoulder of the road so that he could dash over and grab the ball, until suddenly Mr. Mohammadian appeared right next to him and grabbed him by the arm and flung him backward into the open yard. Caleb rolled once, feet over head, before coming to rest on his backside in the wet grass.

He propped himself up on his elbow and peered up at Mr.

Mohammadian, too stunned to move. The man's rough face was wide open with fear and anger, a look that, in a weird way, seemed much more fitting than the distant expression he'd worn only moments earlier. He seemed alert, eager to act. He gestured toward the road behind him. "Are you a crazy person? Do you see the cars? Look at the cars! Look!"

Caleb, still a little dazed, tilted his head to peer around Mr. Mohammadian's legs, toward the lip of the slope. He didn't know what to say. His arm burned mildly from where the man had grabbed him, and his head was still ringing from the roll backward.

The two of them stared silently at each other for some time, until all at once the muscles around Mr. Mohammadian's eyes and mouth relaxed, settling into a guilty frown. There were rules about this sort of thing, Caleb knew, about handling kids who were not your own, and he suspected that Mr. Mohammadian had just violated one of those rules—a fact that seemed to have dawned on the man at that moment—but Caleb understood that it had been an act of instinct, that he had been trying to protect him. "Okay," Mr. Mohammadian said with a sigh, and then he held his hand out for Caleb. Caleb looked at it for a moment and then took it without a word, and he lifted himself to his feet. For a few moments, they stood side by side, staring out to the other side of the highway where the ball had come to rest in the trash-strewn gutter.

Mr. Mohammadian pulled his cigarettes out of his pocket and tapped one out into his palm. "I will get it tomorrow," he said, lighting the smoke.

Caleb looked down at his wet shoes. He felt like he might cry. He wanted to. How many rescues were left? All around him people were going away, Nana and Cassie and now Farhad. None of it made any sense.

"My Nana's sick," he said quietly. It was the first time he'd actually spoken it aloud to anyone other than Cassie, and immediately he felt as though he'd divulged some deep and private truth. It made him feel exposed, skinless. The man looked down at him, the cigarette dangling from the corner of his mouth like an afterthought. Caleb could feel his eyes beginning to glaze over with tears; he couldn't bring himself to meet the man's gaze. "She's got something wrong with her brain. She curses a lot, and she forgets who I am, and she made my sister leave."

"What is wrong with her?"

"I don't know," Caleb replied, shaking his head. "It's a disease." The tears were coming now, strong and hot, and he struggled to steady his voice against his chest's hitching. "But Cassie's gone now and Nana's really mean sometimes and I don't know what to do."

Mr. Mohammadian nodded, exhaling smoke into the cool dark.

"You are afraid."

"Yeah."

He put his hand on Caleb's shoulder. It was the first time in a long while that Caleb could remember anyone touching him, and he twitched slightly as the man's large hand, the rough slab of it, settled upon his collar bone, swallowing up his shoulder. Watching the cars slip past below, Caleb considered that, to any of the drivers down there, they might have looked like a dad and son: two guys playing catch in a yard.

Finally, Mr. Mohammadian flicked his cigarette out into the road, a motion that seemed to signal the end of the conversation. He turned to Caleb. "I have to go inside now." That dreamy, detached quality had returned to his voice, as though he were talking to himself.

Caleb sniffed wetly and wiped his eyes with the back of his arm. "Me too. Home, I mean. I have to go home."

The man turned and loped back across the yard, and Caleb followed. At the front steps he handed the baseball mitt to Mr. Mohammadian, and was about to make his way back around toward the back slope when the man picked up the mix tape from the bottom step and, holding it out in front of him, said, "Do you want me to give this to Reshma?"

The small plastic cassette case gleamed like a jewel in the sallow light of the house, and Caleb realized with a sort of mild shock that he didn't care anymore about getting it to Reshma. It wasn't that he didn't want her to have it; it just didn't seem relevant anymore. Too much had happened since he'd arrived out here, things had changed in a way he didn't quite understand.

Of course, given the efforts he'd taken to make the compilation and then bring it out here, it did seem somewhat futile to take it back home with him, knowing that he would probably just stow it in his desk drawer, and so finally he looked up at Mr. Mohammadian and shrugged and said, "Sure, that's fine."

With this, Mr. Mohammadian nodded in that deep way again, a gesture that seemed to involve his entire upper body, and then turned and slipped back inside the small house. The small brass knocker clacked once, definitively, as he shut the door behind him.

Caleb made his way through the thick wet grass at the side of the house toward the back slope, past the two windows, Reshma's and Farhad's, the latter of which still glowed warmly. When he came to where the chainlink fence met up with the house, he paused and looked out beyond the Mohammadians' back yard to where the ground gave way to the slick, grassy slope. Behind him, the pine trees rustled in the cool breeze. There was something building in him, he could feel it: a feverish need for movement, which he knew was connected somehow to the conversation he'd just had with Mr. Mohammadian, and now suddenly he found himself sprinting along past the back fence, his sneakers kicking up small flurries of wet grass like handfuls of confetti, his fists clenched and his arms working like pistons, running, running, until he finally reached the bottom of the slope, where he sank down into the stiff cheatgrass and, resting his hands on his chest to feel the pulsing of his heart, gazed up at the dark sky, waiting to catch his breath.

The Great American Grill

It was quarter to eleven when the man and the little Asian woman walked into the restaurant. I was the only server on the clock and would be for another half hour or so until the lunch rush started and the rest of the staff arrived. After the hostess had escorted them to table 103, one of the window seats, I stood behind the soda fountain for a few minutes and watched them study the smudgy plastic menus, waiting for the right moment to make my introduction. You don't want to show up at the table too soon; it makes you look overzealous. The trick is to hang back for a while, build up the anticipation a little, like it's going to be something really special. Customers get off on that sort of thing.

I'd been a waiter at the Great American Grill for just over a year at this point. Our theme was The Tastes of America, if you can buy that, which entailed hardly more than a small selection of steaks and sandwiches and a handful of rice-and-bean dishes that the kitchen staff would douse in cayenne and crushed red pepper and then pass off as Cajun. Before coming there I had bartended at a Mexican place that was always playing this jangly mariachi music on the stereo, which made you want to rip your ears off and hurl them across the room. Before that I'd been at this tiny Italian bistro that had actually been pretty decent, pricewise at least, until a few reports of salmonella poisoning surfaced and a couple of old women ended up in the emergency room; that pretty much put the kibosh on the whole place.

After some time I walked over to 103 to get the couple's drink orders. The woman, who I put at about thirty-five, was short and slim with sleek black hair that hung a half inch or so above her shoulders. The man was older, forty or so. He looked like one of these big-shot corporate types from the office parks down the road: black pin-striped suit, oily brown hair that had started to go gray at the temples, and a fake tan that would have been more convincing as a poorly applied coat of wood stain. He ordered a Coke. "Easy on the ice," he added as I walked away from the table, like I had this thing for ice.

They didn't belong together, these two. I couldn't explain it, something was just off about them. That was a strange judgment for someone like me to make, especially in light of the fact that I had just broken things off with my girlfriend, Tess, a manager at the Grill—had, in fact, left her screaming and crying and cursing in the parking lot outside of her apartment complex shortly after midnight two days earlier. But after five years of waiting tables, you develop a sense about these things, people I mean, all their dopey signals. You could see it in the woman's posture, the way she kept her shoulders pressed against the vinyl seatback as though she were posing for a photograph, or how the guy kept looking around the restaurant at the kitschy décor—the early twentieth century Coca-Cola advertisements hanging over the bar, the old black-and-white photos of celebrities that nobody recognized—trying to think of what to say next.

Moments later I returned with their drinks and took out my pad to write down their orders. I didn't need to, of course, not for a table of two—it's just one of these things that make the customer feel special, which, according to the Grill's training video, is *Job One!* The woman spoke with a dry, whispery inflection that was difficult to hear, and I had to ask her to repeat herself to understand that she wanted seafood alfredo. I jotted it down and then turned to the man. "And for you, sir?"

"New York strip." His voice was low and flat and gruff, full of authority. "Rare."

"Medium well is about as good as we can get it, I'm afraid," I said, squinching my face up apologetically. "State law."

"What, like some kind of health code thing?" he said, sneering.

"I guess. I'm not entirely sure. I just know we can't go below mid-well."

He made this sucking sound with his teeth. "Just ask them to get it as rare as they can. I like my steaks to bleed." He flashed the woman a look. She giggled.

I told them their meals would be right up and headed over to the computer to enter their orders. Standing there by the kitchen, I could hear Tess stomping around inside, making a racket. She'd been in a bad mood for the past two days, and she wanted everyone to know it. She was yelling, "*Where the fuck is the blue cheese vinaigrette? Are we out of fucking blue cheese vinaigrette?*"

I knew how this would play out: she'd carry on for another hour or so until she'd made her point, and then she'd go out back by the dumpsters and sit down on the delivery ramp and cry. Someone, one of the prep cooks probably, would step outside to check on her, and would end up sitting through some weepy monologue about what a bastard I was, the general depravity of men, et cetera. Tess knew how to rally people to a cause—this was, in a weird way, one of her more redeeming traits as a manager. By the end of my shift, she'd have half the staff cursing me under their breath. In the meantime, all I could do was try to stay out of her way and go about my business like it was no big deal.

We'd dated for about six months, Tess and I, casually at first, going out to bars together and then coming back and fooling around on her couch, that kind of thing, until around the third month when she'd started staying over at my place regularly and pointing to places in magazines and saying, "We should totally take a trip there." At which point I began to think that maybe things had gone far enough.

After I'd gotten the orders for 103 into the computer, I took a seat in the booth closest to the kitchen, the servers' table we called it. From there you had a panoramic view of the dining room, which allowed you to keep an eye on your tables without having to actively check in with them. I could see the man and the woman, and because there were no other customers in the dining room, I could hear their voices, the man's throaty baritone, the woman's nasally drone. There was a stilted quality to their conversation, like two people at a party who have suddenly found themselves alone. The man was asking the woman whether or not she had any brothers or sisters.

"Two sistah," she replied.

"Here or back home?" he said.

"They back home."

He nodded, clearly racking his brain for a way to follow this up. "I have a sister, too, actually," he said. "She's in Minneapolis. Have you ever been there? To Minnesota?"

"No."

"It's pretty."

The woman shook her head. "Too cold for me."

"I guess it can be. But I like the cold, actually."

As I listened to their stilted dialogue, which even they seemed to sense went on far too long, I couldn't help feeling a little embarrassed for both of them, for the strangeness of the whole thing.

Noel, one of the cooks, shuffled out of the kitchen and took a seat across from me. He was an enormous fellow, three hundred pounds easily, with a patchy red beard and big steel rings in his ears, the kind of guy you befriend out of nothing so much as fear. He pulled a pack of cigarettes out of his grease-stained apron and lit one up and then handed me the pack. He angled his furry chin toward the kitchen where Tess was yelling something about overtime, too many fucking servers milking the fucking clock, and how she wasn't going to take the fucking blame when corporate came to investigate why our labor costs were so high, because she had already told Dennis—the GM—there were already too many fucking people on the fucking schedule, hadn't she?

"How long is she going to keep this up?" Noel said as two thick tendrils of smoke oozed out of his nostrils.

"Don't get me started," I grumbled.

"She's back there reorganizing the goddamn freezer."

"She does that. She reorganizes things. It's a nervous habit."

"I don't know where the hell anything is anymore."

I threw my hands in the air. "What do you want me to do about it? I mean, I can't tell her not to reorganize the freezer, you know."

Noel shrugged and tapped the ash off his cigarette. I could tell that he was a little irritated with me for this whole thing. Pretty much everybody was. It was making work difficult. But what could I do about it? People like Tess don't do clean breaks. She'd made up her mind to be mad, and that's exactly what she was going to do.

Noel and I sat there at the servers' table for some time, smoking our cigarettes and staring lazily out the window at the traffic crawling along Oakley Avenue, all those weary-looking men and women folded up behind the wheels of mid-sized coupes, their faces set into looks of hopeless frustration. After a while Tess stalked out of the kitchen and over to us, her thighs making *fwup-fwup* sounds in her khaki pants. She was a big girl, not fat exactly, *voluptuous* I guess would be the word, like one of those female nudes you see in old Renaissance paintings. She had blond curls that hung down around her thick, babyish face like a gold frame.

"No smoking in the dining room," she said flatly, pointing to my cigarette.

I rolled my eyes. It was an unspoken rule that servers were allowed to smoke at the servers' table so long as their own customers were taken care of. Tess was just looking to break my balls a little. Nonetheless, Noel went ahead and put out his cigarette and then maneuvered his way out of the booth.

After he had waddled back into the kitchen, I looked up at Tess. "There's only one table," I said, pointing to 103. "They're not complaining."

She did this thing she does where she closes her eyes and pinches the bridge of her nose; it was one of her *looks*. "Marty, just put the damn thing out. Don't make me write you up."

I chuckled a little and then stubbed out my cigarette with these real slow and heavy strokes, kind of making a show out of it. Tess wasn't going to write me up; we both knew this. Even if she did, she would never submit it to the district manager. I think the thing that she hated the most about our situation was her inability to take charge of things. "Anything else?" I said finally, dropping the butt into the ashtray.

She sighed. "You really need to grow up. Like, seriously." Then, after a pause: "Your food is up." I slid out of the booth and stood, bumping into her a little. She took a step back and grunted and then stormed off across the dining room, her hands balled into fists at her sides.

To be fair, it wasn't entirely her fault that she was wound so tightly. Her family was a wreck. She'd had an older brother who had died when she was a kid, some kind of bone disease. Her dad was in California and always sent her birthday cards on the wrong day. And her mother was married to this guy Castor, a Jacuzzi salesman with a ponytail.

I went into the kitchen and grabbed the plates from the ledge beneath the heat lamps, and I carried them out to 103. The man and the woman were holding hands across the table like some of those dippy high-school kids who come in from time to time. When they saw me coming, they let go and straightened up in their seats a little and put their napkins in their laps, grinning hungrily. As I set the plates down in front of them, the woman gestured to the man's steak. "Oh, it's big!" she said.

The man chuckled. "Indeed it is."

I was reaching for the small black-pepper mill in my apron when suddenly the woman made this sound that was somewhere between a gasp and a squeak and then leapt out of her seat, nearly knocking me over into the booth behind me. The man looked up at her, startled. "You okay?" he said, but she didn't answer. She stood there, her face wide open with panic, her eyes darting about the room like a frightened animal's. I thought maybe she was going to be sick. The man moved to stand up, but before he was able to the woman dashed across the empty dining room toward the alcove of restrooms in the back. Turning around in his seat, the man watched, puzzled, as she disappeared into the ladies' room, locking the door behind her with a heavy click.

I was still standing there in the aisle beside the table, clutching the pepper mill. "She okay?" I said to the man.

"Don't know," he replied, still angled around in his seat. "Hope so."

That was when the bald man burst through the front doors. Actually, he wasn't completely bald; rather, his head was covered with a fine layer of gray stubble. He had one of those bulky frames you see on guys who've spent most of their lives working with machinery.

The man in the booth—Mr. Wall Street—glanced over at the sound of the doors opening and then muttered, "Goddamnit."

"Sir?" I said.

He slouched down a little in his seat and peered up at me. "Go ahead and bring me the check, will you?"

Over on the other side of the dining room, the hostess, sitting at the bar, dropped her magazine and hustled over to greet the fellow at the door, but before she could unload her smoking-or-non-smoking spiel, the guy said in a terse, husky voice, "I'm looking for my wife, the Cambodian lady."

That was when it all came together for me: the woman's sudden dash to the bathroom, Wall Street slouched down in his seat like a contrite student. Evidently, she had spotted her husband pulling into the parking lot, and so she'd run to the bathroom to hide. The other man, the one she was with, was seated at such an angle to the window that he must not have seen the truck at all.

The hostess looked over at me nervously and, in an uneven voice, said, "Marty?"

The bald guy followed her gaze to 103 and then quickly made his way toward us. His stride was big and lumbering like a gorilla's. But when he got to the table he just stood there, glaring down at Wall Street, who had his arm slung over the maroon seatback, trying desperately to appear aloof.

A few seconds passed, long and dense, before Baldy said, "Hey there." He appeared to be chewing the inside of his cheek.

Wall Street cleared his throat. "Hello."

"How's that steak?"

"Haven't tried it yet."

Baldy nodded thoughtfully. "Why don't you try it?"

"Well, I'm not really hungry."

"Shit, then why'd you order a steak?"

Wall Street looked out the window and sighed, and then looked back up at Baldy. "It seemed like a good idea at the time."

Baldy nodded again and then fell silent. I swallowed anxiously; my throat made a loud clicking sound.

"Go ahead and try it," Baldy continued, gesturing toward the steak. "Just take a bite for me."

Again, Wall Street looked out the window at the parking lot. All of that corporate bravado had drained out of him; now he looked like nothing so much as a frightened kid dressed up in his father's clothes. Sighing, he picked up his fork and knife and cut off a small piece of steak and put it in his mouth and then, with his head lowered, he began to chew slowly.

Out of the corner of my eye, I saw the hostess flit into the kitchen.

Baldy said, "Well?"

Wall Street swallowed, nodding his head. "It's okay."

"Okay? That's it?"

"It's good, but I've had better."

Baldy leaned back and laughed, a single booming *Ha*! that seemed to leap from his mouth like a glob of spit. "I believe that. Yes, I do. I bet you know all about steaks. Probably had your share. I bet you're an expert. Real discriminating taste." The way he said discriminating, it sounded like it had about thirty syllables.

"I don't want any problems, okay?" said Wall Street.

Baldy pretended to be shocked. "Problems? I don't . . . what problems? I'm talking about steaks, is all." He touched the table with the tip of his finger. "Is there a reason for us to have a problem?"

"I don't imagine."

"I mean, I'm just asking about your lunch. If you want to make a problem, we can make one."

Miraculously, it was right then that the hostess returned from the kitchen, trailed by Noel, who wore a look of bafflement that made it clear he had no idea why he'd been summoned, but nonetheless he obeyed the hostess's instruction to take a seat at the bar and keep an eye on 103. He eased his large body down into one of the bar stools and then swiveled around to monitor the scene. He'd done security for a while at a few clubs around town, and he had a way of wielding his presence like a weapon. Baldy looked over at him. Straightening up a little, he took a step back from the table. Wall Street deflated, as though relieved beyond words. Baldy turned to me. He motioned toward the door and said sternly, "I'm going back over there to wait for my wife. I'm not leaving until she comes out, okay?"

He brushed past me and made his way over to the front of the dining room. I took a step after him. "Would you like to wait at a table, sir?" He shook his head and did this quick wave thing with his hand, a dismissive gesture, and continued over toward the door, where he positioned himself next to the hostess podium like a guard.

"Hey," Wall Street croaked. "Check?"

Nodding, I said, "Yes, sir," and then trotted back into the kitchen. I found Tess bent over on the floor of the closet-sized office in the back, trying to reboot the computer, which was about a thousand years old and was prone to freezing up. The tower was underneath the desk; you had to crawl up under it to reach the power button.

"Hey, can you come out front for a minute?" I said.

"I'm busy."

"I think there might be a problem." Her round rear end was sticking out from under the desk, and I couldn't help but notice the outline of her underpants on the seat of her slacks.

She crawled out and sat on her knees. A sweaty clump of hair fell down over her cheek. "What is it?" she said with a sigh.

I explained to her about the couple at 103, about the guy waiting at the door, his wife hiding in the bathroom. Then I led her out into the dining room so that I could point the guy out to her. We stood behind the soda fountain and watched him for a few moments. He was still standing up near the door, scowling down at the floor. The lunch rush had started, and other customers had started streaming in, but the man refused to move. Some of them threw him indignant glances as they edged their way past him up to the hostess stand. The other servers, their arms loaded with plates of food, mumbled, "Pardon me, sir," as they skirted him impatiently. He didn't appear to notice any of it.

"Well, okay," Tess said after we'd ducked back into the kitchen.

"This is a big mess."

"What do you think we should do?"

She shrugged and crossed her arms. "Is there anything we can do? He's not breaking any laws or anything. I could ask him to stand off to the side of the door, I guess."

"How long do you think he's going to wait?"

"Until that chick comes out of the bathroom, probably."

"Exactly. She could be in there for hours."

Tess thought this over. "But she's not breaking any rules, either. I can't kick her out for using the bathroom, Marty."

"She's got the door locked. That could be a problem, depending on how long she stays in there," I said. "Go talk to her."

Tess squinted at me like I was crazy. "What the hell am I supposed to say?"

"I don't know. Charm her. I mean, if this thing gets ugly, you'll be responsible."

She made a face. Dennis wasn't due in until three, which meant that if anything did happen, it was going to happen on Tess's time. She'd had a bad enough week already. I remembered a conversation we'd had a while back in which Tess had tried to convince me that you could tell just from looking whether or not two people in a relationship were truly in love. "It's real subtle," she'd said, "but it's there. You just have to pay attention, you know? It's in the eyes mostly. They have, like, this urgency in them." She was often prone to sentiments of this sort, fleeting romantic spells that always left me feeling tired and squeamish. I suspect this was because her understanding of love had been so mangled by her family, and so maybe she needed to believe that all the mushy nonsense they throw at you in those Sandra Bullock romantic comedies was actually possible, if only to keep herself from going out of her mind.

Now Tess looked up at the ceiling and sighed and then shook her head and said, "Fine." She adjusted the bottom of her shirt, and she trudged toward the ladies room to handle the Cambodian woman.

In the meantime, I printed off Wall Street's check and strode over to the table. He glanced at the tab and then pulled out his wallet and handed me a wad of bills. "Just keep it," he said. I thanked him and told him to have a good one. I was turning to walk off when he reached out across the table and grabbed my wrist. His hand was clammy and warm; it felt like something that had been pulled out of the water on a hook. "Look, I hate to be a problem here," he said in a nervous whisper, "but is there a chance I could use the back door?"

I glanced down at him and then over at the front door where Baldy was keeping his position. Just the thought of helping this man in any way sent a queasy pang through my gut, not to mention that customers really weren't supposed to go in the kitchen (a liability thing). But it was a pretty thick jumble of bills he'd given me, and, to be honest, part of me did feel bad for him, just a little, only because he appeared to understand all too well how outmatched he was. So finally I said, "Okay, let's go."

The cooks glanced up from behind the racks and watched as I led the man through the kitchen and out the back door, onto the delivery ramp, where the sickly sweet stink of the dumpster hung heavy in the warm spring air. "Here you go," I said, motioning to the back parking lot. "You can just walk around front."

But he didn't move, just stood there with his hands on the guardrail, looking out across the garbage-strewn concrete. He was pretty shaken. I wondered what Baldy had made of Wall Street having vanished from the restaurant.

"Husband," he muttered.

"So I gathered," I said.

"She said he was out of town. We were just going to have lunch." He paused and took a breath and then said, "You probably think I'm a huge asshole."

"It's none of my business."

"Yeah, I know. It's just weird, is all. I have this, I don't know. . . I feel like I have to justify it or something. It's ridiculous." He chuckled. "I'm really not that kind of person, I promise. I never even slept with her."

"Really, it's not my business."

I reached for my cigarettes in my apron.

"You got a girlfriend?" he said.

"No," I said. "Well, I'm not sure. It's weird."

He grinned and nodded as though this were a joke. "It usually is, you know?" I didn't say anything.

I stood there on the ramp with him. He gazed pensively out across the back lot like a ship's captain standing on the bow, and I felt the last of my sympathy drain away. I wanted this man gone, far away from my restaurant, far away from me. Finally, a moment later he sighed and said, "Well, thank you again," and then turned and started walking across the parking lot toward the front of the building. His shoes made dainty clicking sounds on the asphalt.

I rested my hands in the large front pocket of my apron, and I felt the wad of cash that he had given me. I pulled it out and counted it. Sixty dollars. The bill had been somewhere around thirty-five.

I stamped out my cigarette and stomped down the ramp after Wall Street, who was rounding the corner of the building when I caught up with him. "Hey," I said, and he turned around and smiled at me. I looked him over for a second, his pressed suit, his electric blue tie, his weak chin obscured by rings of doughy flab. I'm not sure how to describe what it was exactly that I was feeling then, though I can tell you that it was certainly on par with the kind of blind hatred one might feel toward some violent sex offender you read about in the news. I peeled off the extra bills and held them out to him. "You gave me too much."

He looked down at it, frowning. "No, that's for you. I meant to give you that."

"Look, I can't take this. Just . . . here, it's yours." I shook the bills.

"Can't take it," he said to himself, curiously, as though testing the phrase out, and then he took the bills from me and stuffed them into the pocket of his pants. Wall Street wiped his forehead, and I looked down at my shoes. He cleared his throat and then, without another word, turned and walked back around to the front of the restaurant.

I walked back to the delivery ramp and lit another cigarette. Leaning against the railing, I smoked calmly with the hot sun on the back of my neck, listening to the chorus of traffic nearby.

I knew I had other tables to get to inside, but at that moment I didn't care. They could wait a little bit longer. That's really what it all comes down to in restaurants: waiting for someone you don't know to bring you what you want.

By the time I made it back inside, Tess had already managed to coax the woman out of the restroom and was now standing at the front of the dining room looking out through the inner and outer sets of doors toward the parking lot, where the strange couple stood next to the man's truck talking.

"Did he take care of the check?" she asked me, referring to Wall Street. I nodded absently, and then the two of us moved into the little confessional-sized chamber between the two sets of double doors, where the busy clatter of the lunch rush suddenly dimmed to a mild rumble behind us, and we watched, rapt, as the woman, her dark hair glimmering in the brilliant sun, stared up into her husband's hard face with a combination of defiance and guilt—a defendant awaiting punishment. As for her husband, his composure was remarkable. He said something, and the woman responded, and then he nodded solemnly as though she'd just confirmed some sad but inevitable truth. The whole scene was so blindingly calm, so subdued, not unlike the man's exchange with Wall Street only a few minutes earlier. What were we expecting? Tears perhaps, arguing, a performance of sorts. We weren't prepared for the way that they stared at each other, as earnestly as if they were seeing each other for the very first time, and how, with a kind of slow grace, they wrapped their arms around each other, the man having to bend at the waist to reach the woman, and still her head barely made it to his chin, and then they held each other.

"Jesus," Tess said under her breath.

"I know."

"What a mess."

I glanced over at her. The dusty glare of the glass on the other side of her lit her profile with a cool glow. We were alone in there, me and Tess, and it felt good. Peaceful and secure. This was when we were at our best, when it was just the two of us, when there was no world to remind us of how little we had to offer each other. Again I thought about what she had once said about how you can tell just from looking whether or not two people truly loved one another, and I remembered how naïve and childish it had sounded then. Now, though, I don't know, I guess maybe there was something to it, because as I watched the man open the passenger's side door for the woman and then plod over to the driver's side, throwing Tess and me a look—stern but understanding, as if we'd all just lived through something tragic—before climbing inside, I found myself wondering what I might have thought if I had seen them under different circumstances, if I'd seen them in a store or out on the street, somewhere outside the restaurant I mean, where things weren't as familiar, I wondered if I would be able to point them out and say, *You were right, Tess. Look, there it is.*

KISS

$\mathbf{D}$r. Marrus's office is small and white and decorated in a spirit of practicality. No desk, no bookshelf, just two plastic chairs and a host of soft, harmless objects— pillows and stuffed animals and such. Much safer, he says. There used to be a one-way mirror on the wall, so parents could watch the sessions. However, that ended when a ten-year-old caused it to explode, sending a blizzard of glass shards across the next room. Luckily, his parents weren't hurt, though they could have been. Now there are cameras mounted in the four upper corners of the room, each one encased in some fancy polymer coating so the lenses won't be damaged. Doctors have yet to find out why the kids can't breach certain polymers and compounds.

We're here because there is a hole in our kitchen ceiling a foot in diameter.

On the monitors in the next room, Debbie and I watch as a green plush frog hovers in the air, just a few inches from Dr. Marrus's face. He smiles at Elliot's trick, and Elliot returns it, a meager and unconfident grin. This is a good sign. A friendly acknowledgment of praise is a very good sign.

"He smiled at me like that the other day," says Debbie. Her arms are folded across her chest. It makes her look old and frightened.

"Did he really?"

"Lifted my cup out of my hand, held it there—" she makes an imaginary line just in front of her eyes "—for about ten seconds. I smiled at him. He smiled back."

"Big step," I say, not really believing it.

"He's definitely coming around."

The hole was made by our son Elliot, or more accurately, by a large steak knife. It was after this that Debbie and I decided to seek out serious help. We surveyed countless programs, hospitals, and support groups. These days, finding a legitimate parapsychologist that won't bleed you dry is next to impossible. We've invested a fortune in worthless specialists.

So far Dr. Marrus seems decent enough. His name came to us through a newsletter that Debbie had signed us up for shortly before the "knife incident," as we've come to call it. We take Elliot to see him four times a week now. Debbie, though she won't admit it, reveres the man as some sort of medical deity, a shaman, poised to dispel illness with a magic touch. This is the man who is supposed to cure our son, as if Elliot's condition were something as minor as a speech impediment. Me, I'm still at odds with my faith.

The frog circles the doctor's head once, twice, until it falls into a steady spin, around and around, as if attached to an invisible wire. In the monitors Dr. Marrus says something and Elliot turns away. The frog keeps spinning with copter-like precision.

"You'd think he'd have microphones in there or something," I say. Debbie nibbles her fingernails. Dr. Marrus repeats his request and the frog drops to the floor beside him. Its dumb plastic eyes stare at the far wall. Debbie exhales and her body shrinks down a little in her chair. Why she was holding her breath, I have no idea.

～

Our daughter Rene is seventeen. Four years older than Elliot.

For her, Elliot is little more than an unreliable automobile. It's an attitude that frustrates her mother, but I have to admit, there's a part of me that sympathizes with the girl. Other than his vocabulary of meaningless sounds, her brother has never spoken to her, to anyone. Only recently did he begin potty training. Siblings or not, it's an uncomfortable living arrangement for a teenager.

Rene was present for the knife incident. She was standing in the kitchen doorway. She saw the knife rocket upward, the blade—authentic Japanese—break into pieces as it collided with the ceiling, the handle continuing through Elliot's upstairs bedroom and then through the roof, out over the backyard, like the rear half of a spacecraft, careening out of sight. Days later Debbie and I did our best to convince her of the harmlessness of these events, but our fear made the words transparent, and despite our best efforts to minimize what had happened, she understood the seriousness of it. I can't blame her for the way she feels about Elliot.

Over dinner Debbie says, "Elliot smiled at Dr. Marrus again today."

"Great," says Rene.

"It's a pretty big deal, you know. Dr. Marrus says he's making a lot of progress."

"I know."

"You had a test today, didn't you?" I say to our daughter.

"Trigonometry."

"How'd you do?"

"We don't get our grades back until Thursday."

"Were you pretty confident about it?"

"I guess."

"Elliot, quit playing with your food and just eat it," says Debbie. "Here. Your father should have already cut up your steak for you." Rene glances up at Elliot, and then sullenly back down at her plate, barely touched. She has Debbie's eyes—shimmering green eyes that could melt even the most callused heart. Debbie slices Elliot's filet into small cubes. A thick string of drool escapes the corner of his mouth. I lean over to wipe it away with my napkin.

"You know what I dreamt about last night?" I say. "Coffee cups."

"You had a dream about coffee cups," says Rene.

"Yeah. I had all these black coffee cups, and I was trying to clean them out, but each one had a bunch of dirt and cigarette butts encrusted inside. I couldn't get them clean."

"Why were you trying to clean out these coffee cups?" says Debbie, sliding Elliot's plate back in front of him.

"No idea. But there must have been thirty of them. I didn't have a brush or anything, either, just some old faucet."

"That's weird, Dad."

"Yeah, I know. Who dreams about coffee cups, anyway?"

"You do, apparently." Rene smiles at me, lovely and warm. At the other end of the table, Elliot crams small pieces of steak into his mouth with his fingers. His bib is smeared with steak sauce.

~

Dr. Marrus wants to put Elliot on a new medication. We've tried almost everything on the market; before coming to see Dr. Marrus, Elliot went through a parade of medications, none of which had any sort of substantial effect. The drug he wants to give Elliot is called Alvarex. He says it is used for seizures, but some years ago clinical researchers found that it also worked for Telekinetic Disorder—TD. The drug has yet to be approved for such purposes, but Dr. Marrus says that already the medical community is heralding it as a miracle.

"See, up until recently we weren't sure which channels to target in the cerebrum," says Dr. Marrus. "You could give a child all the counseling and all the pills in the world, and you might see some behavioral improvement, but only minimal. Those signals were still getting through those channels and so the child could only progress up to a certain point before just stopping and not getting any better. It's like taking aspirin for a tumor. We call this plateauing." He makes a flattening motion with his hand to demonstrate.

Debbie says, "We're familiar with that."

"Now though, they know which channels to target, so it's just a matter of inhibiting the signal. This'll be huge, and very soon. TD could be completely wiped out, literally. Elliot's problems"—he snaps his fingers—"gone like that."

I feel like I'm at a revival. Any minute now, I'm expecting Dr. Marrus to request a *hallelujah*!

He tells us that he wants to put Elliot on a sustained course of treatment beginning with a year's supply, no charge to us, so long as we agree to a set number of visits during this time. We would also be required to bring Elliot in for occasional blood work and brain tests. He is careful not to use the word "experiment," opting instead for "study." Still, I can't help thinking of beakers and clipboards and stopwatches. I ask him how Alvarex would compare to any one of the failed medications we tried in the past. Very proudly, he states, "Taking it once a day, ninety-seven percent of all subjects tested had significant improvement over two or three months."

"What's 'significant'?"

"Eighty-five percent reduction in all paranormal activity. Those are average figures. In other words, they just weren't able to do it anymore."

I feel Debbie grip my arm tightly. Eighty-five percent. Is that a lot? It sounds like a lot. I don't think to ask the doctor how such a thing can be measured in percentages. Dr. Marrus looks like a game-show host. Debbie's hand is quite cold.

~

By some quirk of brain chemistry, most TD children know what medicine is, and are unwilling to take it. They have instinctive knowledge, not unlike toddlers, that medicine is something foul tasting, foreign, something to be avoided. Doctors do not know why this is, the same way they do not know how they can understand certain words like "mother," "father," and "house" (they have more difficulty with abstract terms like "now," "wrong," and "love"). In the past, Debbie and I had to hold Elliot down while we shoved pills down his throat. I had to clamp his jaw shut with my hand to make sure he swallowed them.

Alvarex are small and yellow and have a chalky texture similar to antacids. This, as Dr. Marrus explains, is so they can be easily broken up and put into food, or dissolved in drinks. That night I grind one into a powder and sprinkle it on Elliot's macaroni and cheese. He doesn't appear to taste it. Watching him eat, one gets the feeling of speeding through a yellow light before it turns red.

Later that night, Debbie and I undress for bed. I look with somber adoration at her figure. In her younger years she had the kind of body that could reduce grown men to hormone-crazed adolescents. Her hips have widened since then, and there are noticeable signs of decreased elasticity in her breasts and stomach. Noticeable, but not unappealing. Actually, there is a degree of respectability in my wife's aging, as if it's something intentional, something that she could reverse at any time, but for reasons more noble than those I could imagine, she chooses not to. It gives her an odd sense of control. I feel my own stomach. It is fleshy and round, speckled with tiny, brittle hairs. Next to my wife I feel unattractive. I feel old and ugly and worn down. I think about what Dr. Marrus said earlier, about plateauing.

"You didn't seem too enthusiastic about the pills," she says to no one in particular.

"I am."

"You're not. I saw that look on your face, Chris. When he told us about Alvarex. You almost looked upset."

"It was a lot to take in, that's all."

"That's a silly thing to say." She slips her nightgown over her head and delicately removes her earrings. They make tiny clinking sounds as she sets them on the nightstand. "Dr. Marrus says he might be able to cure your son and you make it sound like someone just died."

"All this talk of cures. It's a little much, don't you think? What would we be curing, really?"

"We'd be curing Elliot, Chris. We'd be curing his condition. We'd be making it so we can all feel more safe and comfortable, so Elliot might have the kind of life he deserves."

"He'll never have a normal life."

"I didn't say he would. But he won't be launching cutlery through the ceiling anymore."

"He still won't be able to speak."

"But he might be able to learn how."

"How do we know he can't now? Maybe he just doesn't have anything to say."

"You are unbelievable." She leans over and sets the alarm on the clock radio. The numbers glow angrily, a deviant red. "Turn out the light. I'm tired."

~

The following Saturday I play racquetball with Bill Ballard. We play once a week. I came to know Bill through one of the support groups Debbie and I joined a few years back. He's a smart fellow, a tax attorney who coaches little league soccer, though not much of a racquetball player. His daughter makes things vibrate. It's usually harmless, but every so often something gets damaged, a door frame or a piece of furniture. Bill has to keep a seismograph in his bedroom.

"Alvarex," he says. "Seizure medicine, right? Yeah, I remember reading an article about it."

"They're still testing it for other uses. The FDA still has to approve it before doctors can prescribe it. This is part of the study."

"And you're putting it in his food?"

"Yes."

"I see. Well, if you think it can fix Elliot, then what's the problem?"

"I'm not sure. I'm just not crazy about rushing to fill my kid full of medicine."

"Yeah, but if it's helpful . . ."

"That's just it. Alvarex only affects the part of the brain that sends and receives the signals. So even if Elliot stops making things fly across the room, he's still a kid who can't talk, read, speak, have any sort of relationship. You know what I mean?"

"Chris, I'm not sure. I might have to side with Debbie on this one. Think about people who wear glasses. What's the difference? Glasses don't make people smarter, but they do make things more convenient."

"True. But take blind people. Their other four senses are much better than yours or mine."

He sighs. "Elliot isn't blind, Chris. He's mentally incompetent."

I feel a slight sting of offense at this statement, but Bill is usually right about these things. Just look at his daughter. Ten weeks without an incident, and that's with no medication whatsoever, just biweekly counseling. Pretty outstanding, really. As for Elliot, he's only been seeing Dr. Marrus for two weeks and already the atmosphere in the house feels much less frantic. And maybe that's what has me so tense, this calm streak. I'm not used to it. It's like amputees who lose an arm and say they can still feel their fingers.

Later that night I hear Rene thudding down the stairs. She trots into the TV room and asks if she can borrow the car for a few hours.

"What did your mother say?"

"She's giving Elliot a bath," she says. "She told me to ask you."

"All right then. My keys are on my dresser. Be back by midnight." When she turns to leave the room I call her back. "Between you and me, how do you think your brother is doing?"

She leans over the counter and her hair spills over her shoulders. When she was born her hair was red and curly. Then, at some point during her infancy, it turned dark. It makes me think of all the sad, pretty girls I used to ache for in college.

"I'm really glad you guys put him on those pills. Seriously."

"You think they're helping?"

"Absolutely."

"And you don't think we're lousy parents for putting it in his food, do you?"

"No. You couldn't get him to take it otherwise. It's the only way."

When she's gone I climb the stairs to find Debbie. I see her kneeling over the bathtub, scrubbing the basin. Hard, deliberate arm movements across the white porcelain. There is a sour quality about the air in here. Elliot is naked on the floor by the sink. He sits Indian-style and rocks back and forth in time to the metronome that ticks continuously in his head. I smile at him. He says, "Gah!"

I kneel behind my wife and wrap my arms around her stomach. "Elliot had an accident," she says. Her body is soft and warm. I nestle my face in her neck. Her hair is wispy and smells like peaches. Her skin is moist with sweat, and when I kiss her I taste the remnants of some fragrant and exotic lotion. "Could you go get me the bleach from downstairs?"

"Sure."

As I walk out of the bathroom I stop and ruffle Elliot's damp hair. "Make a mess there, pal?" He brings his hands together in a haphazard motion similar to clapping. Again he says, "Gah!"

I was slicing up a tomato at the counter. Debbie was at the sink. I turned to face her, to answer a question she'd asked me—I don't recall what—and that was when I felt the knife leave my hand. It glided out of my grip and hung there in front of me for a moment, almost indecisively, before tearing through the ceiling. Chunks of tile and debris and serrated stainless steel clattered to the floor. Debbie and Rene, who was standing in the kitchen doorway, shrieked and covered their heads.

For some reason, none of us had noticed Elliot standing behind Rene.

Of all the things in the kitchen, all those appliances, dishrags, food, the coffee and sugar canisters, the cleaning supplies under the sink, it was the knife he chose. Or was it the case that he didn't choose it at all? It seemed too sinister a move for our boy. Is it possible to make a choice and not know it? Your heart keeps beating even when you're not thinking about it. That was the looming question afterward: are these acts a conscious effort on his part, or have we overestimated his control? Neither option was any more or less frightening than the other.

Rene stumbled backward out of the room and bolted up the stairs. The walls shook with the slamming of her bedroom door. Debbie crouched down in front of Elliot. She grabbed him just above his elbows and howled into his face, "Elliot, stop it! You do not do that! That is dangerous!" Her voice rang out like copper.

And me? I just stood there by the counter, my fingers dripping with tomato juice. I looked up through the hole in the ceiling, through Elliot's room and then outside. The sky was a passive gray. The next day I contacted my insurance company. Then I called Bill Ballard.

As far as my wife and daughter are concerned, Elliot's vocabulary does not extend beyond gurgling, monosyllabic outbursts and the occasional string of incoherent syllables. And even that is only when he is very upset. However, he did speak once, only once, and only one word, but after thirteen years of "gah" and "bip" and "erp," that one word contained unthinkable depths of information.

This was several months prior to taking him to Dr. Marrus, before the damage in the kitchen and the upstairs ceiling. Debbie was at a baby shower. Rene was at a friend's house. I sat on the sofa watching TV while Elliot lay on the floor in his pajamas, cooing endearingly to the congregation of stuffed toys scattered about. He rolled onto his side and looked up at me, his forehead lined with sharp creases, his mouth taut. There was an alertness about him I'd never seen.

"Kiss!"

I recoiled, as one would do at the sound of a nearby gunshot. My first thought, as I remember, was of Debbie, of how delighted she would be, and I had the briefest glint of speculation as to the guilt she'd feel for having missed it. I knelt down beside him. He was sitting up by this point, rocking, like usual. He said it again. "Kiss!"

I kissed him on his forehead. This made his expression stiffen a little. I had frustrated him in some way. He pressed a crooked finger into my chest, hard and full of intent.

"Kiss!"

We looked at each other. Nothing.

"Kiss!"

And right then the strength evaporated from my legs and I fell onto my rear. I landed in a sitting position in front of him. Something clenched in my chest like the cogs of some large and complex machine springing to life. My nerves opened like blossoms.

Chris. He was saying "Chris." He was saying my name.

My son knew how to say my name.

Slowly, I reached out and touched his shoulder. "Elliot."

His finger dug into my shirt, my skin. "Kiss!"

"Elliot."

"Kiss!"

How long did it last? Seconds only, but it felt like years. Easily the heaviest handful of moments of my life. How had this happened? What did it mean, if anything? All I could do was sit there on the carpet, my gaze locked securely into my son's face, hoping with something of a panic that he'd say something else, anything, one more word, a smile even, some sign that he, too, understood the gravity of the situation. But nothing came. Instead, he rolled clumsily back onto the floor and continued chirping at his toys.

Why I didn't tell the rest of my family about this development, I don't know. Perhaps I envisioned Elliot on the monitor at Dr. Marrus's place, colorless and stale. Maybe I imagined Debbie carrying him off in a reckless dash, the eagerness she'd feel as she waited for the good doctor to coax something else out of him, and her disappointment when it didn't come. Because somehow I knew it would be the only time he spoke, the same way you can know that someone's looking at you when you're facing the other way. It was my name he said, mine, and whether or not it was selfish—I'm not sure—that kind of intimacy was too important, too fragile to reveal. To let anyone else in on what had happened would corrupt it, I thought. It didn't feel right to tell my wife or my daughter. It felt like betrayal.

~

Dinners now are sullen and unsettling. An element of artificiality has crept in now that Elliot is unknowingly taking Alvarex. We eat mostly in silence, pretending not to watch as he shovels heaps of food into his face. Our conversations are forced, inauthentic, cheap appeals to normalcy that to someone like Dr. Marrus would probably come across as textbook dysfunction. Nothing out of the ordinary here, see? Just an average American family. You could frame us and hang us on a wall. We always make sure Elliot completes his meal first.

~

The contractor is a stocky bearded man named Hal. Bill Ballard recommended him to me, which is the only reason I've waited two weeks for the man to finish up another job before coming out to give us an estimate. He stands in the kitchen with his hands on his hips, craning his neck to examine the hole in the ceiling.

"Looks like you got a busted rafter," he says. "I'll have to patch that. You're lucky it didn't hit any wiring. That hole's only a few inches from the light fixture there. You say a knife did this?"

"My son did it. With a knife."

"Geez. Poor kid."

We look at the damage upstairs in Elliot's room, where the knife barely missed the rafters. Again Hal tells me how lucky I am. He says he'll still have to replace the plywood sheathing and roof shingles. About two grand for the whole thing.

"How long?"

"Two, three days," he says.

The front door closes. Rene skulks up the stairs, dragging her bookbag by one of the straps.

"Hey, sweetie."

"Hi."

"You look tired."

"I am."

Teenagers always have this wonderful air of desperation about them, as if they are the pioneers of heartache.

"Did you have dance-line practice today?"

"Yeah."

"How was it?"

"It was okay," she says with a shrug. Her bedroom door closes and a moment later I hear the atonal pulsing of some rock band. I think about all the books I've read about kids like Elliot, all the brochures and magazine articles. Troubleshooting manuals for faulty brains. I wish they made those for the rest of us.

Meanwhile, Hal stands on his toes in Elliot's room, inspecting the punctured ceiling. I pretend not to see him pick his nose and wipe his finger on the front of his blue work shirt. He says, "We had this job one time, family of five, kid like this," he motions to the hole above us. "Kid got mad one night, who knows why, and set fire to his room. Just like that, just standing there. I tell you, that whole damn room was scorched, top to bottom. Whole section of the house had to be torn down and rebuilt. Messy business."

"Jesus."

"Yep. Come to find out they finally put him in a hospital up-state, you know the one I'm talking about? Put him up there, didn't have no more problems. They go see him every couple of weeks. Too bad he's so far away, but like the boy's daddy said, he's got the rest of his family to look after, you know? He said, at least nobody got hurt."

"Absolutely."

"Coulda been a lot worse."

"I know."

Overhead in the twelve-inch circle of sky, a jet passes, leaving behind a milky stream of smoke.

~

I drive home along slick asphalt roads, past too-quaint boxy houses. Ordinary folks live here, grocery baggers and teachers and mechanics, old veterans forever grumbling about Social Security, mothers and fathers and aging relatives, people with well-manicured little lives. A demonstration in complacency. The whole thing is wrapped in a sense of prearrangement, carefully laid out like an exhibit, as if things look this way not by chance, but because they were always meant to. Roads lead into more roads. Leaves fall.

For some reason, I think of Elliot's ultrasound. I think about Debbie lying on her back, and I remember the large white dome of her belly. I remember the two of us staring at the screen next to her bed, at the blue-gray image of our son, bent up on himself as if in some ascetic position of worship. "A boy, Chris," she said. "A little boy." I smiled. The image flickered and fizzled, and then the screen went blank. The doctor didn't even bother checking the equipment. He didn't have to. Debbie gripped my arm the way she did in Dr. Marrus's office the day he told us about Alvarex. I suppose it's better we found out then instead of later on.

I pick up dinner: take-out Italian in black styrofoam containers. At home Debbie is reading aloud to Elliot, who appears to be absorbed in a soundless dialogue with a plastic spoon. I set the bags of food on the kitchen counter. "I got that pasta you like," I say to Debbie.

"The one with the chicken?"

"The one with the chicken."

Elliot makes a giddy squealing sound. Debbie chuckles. I ask her where Rene is.

"Upstairs. Go tell her to wash her hands for dinner. I'll get him ready." She motions to Elliot. "And grab the you-know-what from the bathroom."

I knock on Rene's door and tell her to wash up. Through the abysmal racket of her stereo I hear her say okay. In the bathroom I run my hands under the faucet and grab the bottle of Alvarex off the sink basin. The bottle is a frank transparent brown, and the pills rattle happily as I walk down the stairs. Like candy, I think to myself.

While Debbie struggles to put Elliot's bib on him (I think he secretly knows how much it irritates his mother when he jerks around like this) I empty the containers onto dinner plates. The kitchen swells with the earthy smells of garlic and basil and oregano. I open the pill bottle and shake one out into my hand. When I see Debbie trot into the other room to turn off the television, I swallow it.

It goes down stubbornly, sticking in my throat for a moment, leaving a gooey trail of residue on my tongue. I can see why Elliot would refuse it. When I turn around, it is not Debbie I see but Rene, standing in the doorway, her eyes fixed on me, her face something of a scowl, but then again, she's always scowling. For a few seconds we stand there like this, not really sure if we're supposed to feel as awkward as we do. Debbie reenters the kitchen. She shoves a plate of food into Rene's hands. Angel hair in a white wine sauce. I turn away. I feel like I've just walked in on a stranger in a public restroom.

Just above me, the hole in the ceiling looms like an open mouth.

I'm lucky it didn't hit any wiring.

Elliot babbles at his green plastic juice cup while I say grace. We pick through our meals methodically. Rene twirls strands of pasta around her fork. My wife takes her eyes off our son only long enough to take in tiny bits of food. She winks at me, a gesture that makes me feel hollow. I watch Rene eat. I wait for her to look at me, to acknowledge our moment in the kitchen. Her eyes never leave her plate. Lately her eating habits have taken on a seething formality that seems somehow appropriate for a girl in her position. Meals are a chore. Her family is an exercise in tolerance. Her life is a lonely satellite of a much larger, much more prosperous world. Everything is predictable, temporary, without impact. My daughter doesn't look anything like me.

We call this plateauing.

Debbie leans over to wipe globs of red meat sauce off of Elliot's face. "You're making a mess, mister." She rubs her hand over his head, smoothing back his hair. His fingers dance like reeds blowing in a gentle wind. Our son. My son. Look at him. His name is Elliot and he has blue eyes and brown hair and one time he said my name. One time he said Chris. Debbie presses her lips to his forehead. It makes a wet smacking sound. Elliot doesn't seem to notice. He says, "Gah!"

The Shed

For Gilbert Dexter

My brother James called me one night to suggest we drive over to our parents' house to clean out our father's tool shed. This was in mid-August, three months after Dad's passing. He had dropped dead of a heart attack one afternoon while trimming the weeds at the side of the house. A neighbor had spotted him lying on the ground by the fence, the weed whacker still rumbling around in the grass beside him. "It's not like Mom has any plans for it," James said, referring to the contents of the shed. "You know it's just going to sit there and rust. We should at least do something with it."

I didn't particularly feel up to the task, only because I hadn't really felt up to anything since the funeral. In fact, this would have been the first time in several weeks that I'd left my apartment for anything more than another stack of frozen dinners from the grocery store down the road, where the cashiers had come to regard me with the kind of brittle tolerance usually reserved for homeless people. But I knew that James was right about Mom forgetting everything in the shed. Since Dad had died, she'd gone out of her way to avoid the house in favor of the church, where she would busy herself for most of the day with inane little tasks—dusting the hymnals in the pews, buffing the floors of the Sunday school rooms—mired in a state of severe denial. And as much as I hated the idea of peeling myself out of my apartment to clean out my dead father's things, the thought of all his tools being left out there to rust bothered me even more. So, the following Saturday afternoon I picked James up in my truck and we headed to our folks' house.

The shed was little more than a large wooden cube set up on cinder blocks in the back yard by the fence. It was crammed full old cobwebby tools, rusted-over cans of paint, and pieces of rotten lumber, all left over from Dad's post-Navy years when he'd worked briefly as a general contractor. We started by hauling the table saw and some of the other bulkier items out into the yard to free up space inside. The smaller pieces, hand tools and such, we tossed unceremoniously out into the overgrown grass to be sorted out later.

In the back corner was an old mildewy tarp, tucked beneath a long plywood shelf running the length of the far wall. It had been weighted down with a few bags of instant concrete that had long since hardened into big stone lozenges. I hefted them off to the side and pulled back the tarp to find sixteen sloppy stacks of old pornographic magazines, their covers gnarled and wrinkled and faded with age.

I called James in from the yard where he was sorting through a box of old drill bits, and I led him over to the magazines. For a while all we could do was stand there trying to make sense of what we were seeing, until finally James chuckled and said, "Wow." He grinned as if I'd just told him a dirty joke. "Did you know about this?"

"No. You?"

He shook his head. "But I guess it's better we find out this way instead of, you know, some other way."

He hunkered down and began to rifle through the magazines. There had to be at least two hundred of them, the titles ranging from recognizable (*Penthouse, Hustler*) to pointedly obscure and artless (*Horny Housewives, Xtreme Asian Teens*). The women leered back at us from the warped pages, their sleek, pliant bodies sprawled across enormous beds or draped over the hoods of expensive automobiles. They wore stringy lingerie and thick coats of oil that gave them the appearance of having been basted—ready to be devoured. There was a fairly predictable gamut of costumes, cowgirls and French maids and nurses; in one picture, a pantyless Dorothy Gale lay on her back in a field of poppies with her gingham skirt bunched up around her waist, while a man dressed as the Tin Man knelt before her with her ruby slipper-clad feet propped up on either of his shoulders, as though he were peering through a set of prison bars. His costume amounted to nothing more than a full-body coat of silver paint and a small funnel strapped to his head.

"Jesus," James cackled. "I can never watch that movie again."

I stumbled out into the yard and braced myself against the table saw.

James appeared in the doorway of the shed. "You okay?" he called, still laughing a bit.

"I just need a minute."

"Take your time," he replied, and then disappeared back inside the shed, presumably to continue pawing through the magazines.

I stood there for a few minutes with my hands planted on the edge of the cutting board and my head hanging down between my shoulders, trying to collect my thoughts. I knew I was experiencing something like shock. How long had this been going on? What drives someone to cultivate such a collection? No one likes to think of their father as a person with secrets. I remembered the time back in seventh grade when Vince Doss and I had gotten caught watching a bootlegged copy of *Lipstick Lesbians*; Vince had forgotten to take the tape out of the VCR and his parents had discovered it and called my folks (James had found this infinitely amusing). Dad was furious, more than he should have been, I considered as I sat on the stool in the kitchen listening to him howl at me for a good twenty minutes about how Vince, whom he confessed to having always thought of a bad seed, and I should know better, how we were too young for that kind of thing, on and on, until finally he grounded me for a month.

Now this. I didn't know what to make of it, all these magazines. It was a phenomenal leap in logic, one that my brain seemed almost incapable of making.

Mom was at the church helping to prepare the parish hall for a wedding reception. She wasn't supposed to be home until around five, but it was still pretty weird having the magazines out in the open like that, so we dumped them into black garbage bags and stashed them behind the woodpile for the time being.

The rest of the afternoon we spent in near silence, rummaging inside the musty shed, our clothes dark and heavy with sweat. We decided to skip lunch so we could knock it all out as soon as possible. I watched James stroll back and forth between the yard and the shed with the broad, confident gait of a man who has recently come into privileged information, his mouth puckered in a cocky smirk. At thirty-six—three years older than me—he bore a remarkable resemblance to our father: same jowly cheeks, same hefty frame. The fuzzy pale crescent of his belly peeked out from beneath his faded Redskins' t-shirt.

James was someone you had to get used to, the kind of guy who whistles at girls and never picks up the tab. He'd been the general manager of an outer space-themed restaurant up until a year earlier when a nineteen-year-old waitress filed a sexual harassment claim against him. He'd sworn up and down that he never laid a finger on the girl, but they canned him all the same. Since then he'd been working in a Best Buy warehouse not far from our folks' place. It was only temporary, he'd told me, just until he got his feet back on the ground, but as far I could tell he wasn't rushing to make any plans.

I was teaching statistics at a nearby community college at this time, not a huge step up from what my brother was doing, at least not financially, but I perceived it as a variation on what I had set out to do. I lived in a tiny one-bedroom apartment near the school, in a complex populated primarily by Mexican immigrants. I had a cat and an exercise bike and a 36-inch television. Weekends were spent going to the movies by myself and wondering what my next move was supposed to be.

In a way, I had hoped that Dad's passing might offer some sort of perspective on things, one of those life-affirming epiphanies you see in Frank Capra films. This was what had been going through my head during those last few days in the hospital, which I had spent dozing in the stiff armchair next to the old man's bed, listening to the hiss of the oxygen machine and watching his skin take on the pallor of uncooked chicken; I kept thinking that maybe I was supposed to be learning something from all this.

††

It was close to four by the time James and I finished with the shed. Peeling off our damp t-shirts, we shambled out into the yard and sat in the grass, muttering *Geez* and *Oh man* and rubbing the backs of our necks. James trotted inside the house and returned a moment later with two beers. We sat in the shade with our backs against the shed, drinking in silence, too worn out to make conversation. When I'd finished, I sat my bottle on a scrap of particle board lying nearby and motioned toward the bags behind the woodpile. "We should get these to a dumpster," I said. "We can sort out the rest of this stuff later on. I don't want Mom to see them."

"Hang on a sec," said James. He stood slowly, wincing at the clicking sound of his knees, and walked over to the bags. With his cigarette in his teeth—something he'd picked up from Dad, a pack-a-day smoker up until the end—he kneeled down and fished around inside of one.

"You know, some of this stuff is pretty old," he said.

"So?"

"So, what I'm saying is that there's, like, a market for that sort of thing. Vintage pornography."

I stood and walked over to him. "You're not serious."

"Look. Some of these go back to, like, the sixties. I mean, check this out." Reaching into the bag, he dug out a small magazine and handed it to me. The cover featured the grainy image of a plump blonde in lacy black underwear lounging sideways in a big Victorian-style armchair with her fishnet-bound legs hanging lazily over the armrest, a small black stiletto dangling from her toes like some kind of threat. The date on the spine was 1964, nine years before I was born. This meant that either Dad had been into this stuff since his thirties, or that it was something he'd picked up later on. Neither possibility was any less disturbing.

James stood and flicked his cigarette into the yard. He tapped the cover of the magazine. "See what I mean? Very retro, am I right?" The way he said retro, it wasn't so much a word as a sound, something low and croaky, like a broken video reel.

I handed the magazine back to him. "I don't know if this is old enough to be considered vintage."

"Like you're an authority."

"How do you know that people are into this?"

He shrugged. "I mean, you just hear about it, you know? People are into all sorts of weird shit. I think I read something about it on the internet."

That my brother might know a little about vintage pornography didn't exactly surprise me. I confess that when the sexual harassment allegations had first surfaced, I wasn't sure what to believe. It would be nice to say that I had instinctively leapt to his defense, but the truth is that it didn't strike me as something totally out of character for him.

James' plan was to carry the magazines out to the Tropic of Cancer, an adult bookstore a couple blocks from Uncle Tim's house out in Ghent—a good twenty-minute drive from Mom and Dad's place. As I thought it over, I couldn't help feeling that there was something mildly insensitive about pawning off Dad's stuff so easily. Giving tools away was one thing, but this was something else entirely, a secret, something that no one was supposed to know about, not even us, and with this in mind, the idea of profiting from the magazines felt a little sinister.

Of course, this was all assuming that the store was even willing to take the magazines, which, given their condition, didn't seem likely. I figured, worst case scenario, the place refused, and we ended up tossing them in a dumpster somewhere. We'd be getting them off our hands either way, but at least this way we got a long air-conditioned drive in my truck, and after huffing around in the sun all day, this actually sounded pretty good.

And so finally I agreed, and James went inside the house to call the place to ask about their buyback policy on used magazines. A few minutes later he walked out to the driveway where I was loading the bags into the back of the truck, and he pumped his fists in this lame little thumbs-up dance. "The guy said to bring them on out," he announced.

I hopped down off the tailgate and wiped the sweat from my forehead. "Dad would be thrilled."

He waved his arm dismissively. "Lighten up, Professor. This is the silver lining of a very dark cloud. We should at least try to make the best of it."

††

As we swung out onto the highway, James asked me if I thought Mom suspected anything about the magazines.

"Absolutely not," I replied. "Obviously he was trying to hide the stuff. Otherwise, why would he keep it in the shed?"

"I guess." James stared thoughtfully out the window. I'd believed him when he told me he hadn't known about the magazines, but now it occurred to me that I wouldn't have been surprised either way. "We're not going to tell her, are we?" he said after a few moments.

"Who? Mom? No, we're not going to tell Mom. Jesus. Why would you want to do that?"

"I didn't say I wanted to, I was just asking if we were going to."

"The answer is no."

"You don't think maybe she has a right to know?" There was a snide quality to his voice, something lawyerish and suggestive, like he was baiting me.

I sighed. "You know it's not an issue of rights, James. Mom's got enough on her mind right now without having to deal with the fact that her late husband was a sexual deviant."

"Doesn't make him a deviant," he replied coldly.

"You know what I mean."

For a moment he just eyed me with this narrow sideways scowl, the same look that Dad used to give us as kids when we'd gotten out of line, and then he turned his attention back out the window. In the distance we could see the Norfolk shipyards looming like the ruins of some war-torn cityscape with its huge grey hulls and its jumble of control towers. We passed the Jamaica

Tavern, an old topless bar that was owned by one of Dad's friends from the local chapter of the Naval Officers' Association. I could remember the time years earlier when the man had contracted Dad to build a new runway for the main stage. There was an issue with termites, he'd explained, and he didn't need some poor dancer falling through the wood and breaking an ankle. On a Saturday afternoon in December of my senior year of college, Dad loaded me and James and Mom into the van and hauled us over to the club to see the runway he'd constructed. He ushered to us to a table at the front of the room, which was lit almost exclusively by these tiny bamboo lamps on each of the tables, past a half dozen or so sullen, disheveled characters who peered up at us skeptically, as though awaiting a punchline. The runway, carpeted with a dark blue nylon flatweave, jutted out from the semi-circled main stage toward the center of the room, approximating a crude phallic shape that wasn't immediately noticeable, not unless you'd taken a good look at the plans. Sipping his beer, Dad ran his hand across one of the three-foot mirrors paneling the sides of the structure. "Look here," he said dreamily as a dark-skinned girl in a red see-through teddy strutted past our table. "Can't even see the framing. See? Yeah, that's gonna hold up real good." The girl glanced uneasily toward our table, more at Dad it seemed, which angered me in a way that I didn't really understand, even though he didn't seem to notice her at all. Mom stared down into her iced tea as though she wanted to crawl inside of it.

††

The Tropic of Cancer was a small brick building in the back corner of a weedy lot nestled amongst a strip of glum warehouses and machine shops. The inside was surprisingly bright, lit by long tracks of fluorescent lights running the length of the paneled ceiling. A portly gray-haired fellow stood behind a dusty glass counter by the door with his chin in his hand, staring down at a book of crosswords. He looked up at us we entered and then immediately back down at his puzzle. James approached the man and introduced himself. "I called a little while ago? About the magazines?" He jerked a thumb toward me, hovering behind him. "This is my brother Dave."

The man reached across the counter and gave James' hand a quick pump. "Stan."

James bobbed his head in greeting and then shoved his hands in his pockets. For a few moments we just stood there, me and him, not really sure where to go from here, until finally Stan sighed and stood up straight and said, "Well, show me these magazines, then."

There were no customers in the store at the moment, so he followed us outside to the truck. James led him around to the back and dropped the tailgate and then lit a cigarette and stood off to the side and watched as Stan sorted through the collection of crusty magazines. He picked up a copy of *Barely Legal*, flipped halfway through, dropped it back into the garbage bag. The pages made a crunching sound like dead leaves. "Hell of a collection here," he said in a way that might have been sarcastic, though the flat, stiff timbre of his voice made it hard to tell.

"They were our dad's," James said. I flashed him a look; I didn't like him broadcasting this fact to strangers. He rolled his eyes at me.

After a few minutes Stan shoved his hands in his pockets and stepped back from the truck, and I noticed for the first time that he was wearing a t-shirt from the local chapter of the Naval Officers' Association. He'd been leaning against the counter inside so that the emblem on the front—a small gold anchor encircled by five hands, affecting a pentagon—hadn't been noticeable. Dad had had a shirt exactly like it, though this didn't really mean much; all of the retired sailors in the area did. But still. I guess I was just in the position to draw connections.

Clearing his throat, Stan fixed his droopy gaze upon us. "Yeah, well, I mean, I'll take them if you're just gonna throw them out. There's always someone who'll want them."

"Okay. How much?" said James.

Stan cocked his head. "How much what?"

"Money. How much were you willing to spend?"

The man's eyes went wide. "What, you want me to *buy* this stuff?" A jagged laugh crept up out of his throat. "It don't work that way at all."

But James wouldn't be deterred. He just kept smiling in that self-assured way he had, like he knew something you didn't. Haggling got him all worked up; he liked to think of himself as crafty and shrewd, someone to be dealt with.

"Come on now, hold up. There's some good stuff in here. Look at the dates. See? That's classic, man. Vintage, know what I mean?"

"No resale value," Stan said calmly. "Half this stuff's ruined, can't hardly turn the pages. Mint condition, maybe I could help you out, but the way it is, all I can do is give you some store credit."

"How much?"

With a contemplative groan, Stan once again reached down into the bag and sifted through the amalgam of stiff, sticky pages. He scratched his neck. "Twenty."

"That's it? Twenty?"

"Yup."

A peculiar twinge of defensiveness ran through me. An hour or so earlier I'd been trying to convince James that the magazines were more or less worthless. But now, to hear it from someone else, someone who didn't know Dad, it was hard not to feel a bit slighted on my father's behalf.

All the same, I knew that this was a pretty generous offer. However trivial this favor of Stan's might have been, it was still a favor. I looked up at James, standing on the opposite side of the truck with his arms folded on the top of the bed wall, and I shrugged and said, "We're already here. It's not like anyone else is going to want them."

James tossed his cigarette butt out into the parking lot. "Yeah, okay."

Moments later we got to work moving the bags into a small musty stock room at the back of the store. Stan stood behind the counter, hunched over his puzzle booklet, watching us plod back and forth from the truck to the room. A couple times I caught myself staring at his shirt, the front of which was partially visible over the lip of the counter. Dad had worn his whenever he'd worked in the back yard, and I had this image of him tromping around out around the shed, his faded jeans sagging against the weight of his leather tool belt—a Father's Day gift from James and me.

When we were finished with the magazines we ambled up to the counter, and Stan looked up from under his thick grey brow and said, "That it?"

"That's it," James replied.

The man swept a hand through the air like a model on a game show, gesturing toward the plastic white racks of merchandise behind us. "Twenty bucks. Go crazy."

Well, now this was a decision. James and I turned and looked out over the shelves of shrinkwrapped magazines and DVDs. I felt like I was trying to solve a kind of puzzle, only I had no idea where to begin.

"You can go pick," I said to James.

"You sure?"

"Yeah, go ahead," I replied. I figured James was the authority on the subject, and anyway, he was the one who'd brokered the deal. "It's not really my thing," I said. "I wouldn't know where to start."

As James made his way over toward the racks, I walked back to the counter and leaned against it. Stan glanced up at me from his booklet. I pointed at his shirt. "You serve?"

He nodded slowly. "Korea, fifty-one to fifty-three."

"Our dad was in Korea. Kirk Baumgardner?" I'd heard stories of retired soldiers coming across men they'd served with years earlier, in bars or grocery stores. It wasn't common, but in a city so crammed with retired servicemen, it certainly wasn't unheard of.

But Stan shook his head in that slow, uneasy way of his and said: "Never heard of him." He looked back down at his booklet and scribbled in a couple of letters and then said, "He make it through okay?"

"Yeah, he made it." I fingered one of the novelty lighters on the counter, a woman's torso, minus limbs, with tiny red lights for nipples that lit up when you pressed the silver button at the top. "How long have you had this place?"

He glanced up at the ceiling, thinking it over. "Bought it in seventy-one, so that's—thirty-seven years."

"Long time."

"I suppose."

I glanced over at James, who was examining the back of a DVD case. He seemed like he was halfway across the world at that moment. "Hey," I said to Stan in a near-whisper, like we were trading secrets, "let me ask you something."

Before I could get the question out, Stan looked up at me head-on with those grim grey eyes of his and he sighed heavily through his nose and said, "You wanna know why this kind of place? Is that what you wonna ask?" His voice had a hard edge to it that made me lean back a little. "Why pornography?"

"You got me," I replied, smiling, but it was too transparent, too desperate.

"That's what everyone wants to know. That's what they all ask."

"I wasn't trying to be rude or anything. I was just curious."

Stan set his pencil down on the dingy counter, slapped it down really, a gesture that spoke of countless other conversations like this one. It was that type of defensiveness that over time builds up in those people who are, for one reason or another, constantly expected to explain themselves, until soon enough it becomes a part of their character, a kind of tic. Immediately I wished I hadn't asked the question. "Look, I got four kids from two different marriages." he said sourly. "I ain't gotta tell you that's a lot of money. But this is a solid market. I mean, I've seen businesses come and go all over this area. Somebody opens a store or a bar or something, they stick around for a few months, then one day there's a sign in the window and a chain around the door handles."

I leaned back a little. "I honestly didn't mean anything by it. I was just curious—"

"But see, that ain't a problem with places like this, you know?" he continued as if he hadn't even heard me. "Everybody's into something, even if they won't admit to it. And they always will be. There's a reason the porn industry brings in five billion a year. I get people trying to shut me down, churches and protesters and whatnot, but they're the same ones what keep me in business. They just don't like to admit it. I figure, let them. I ain't going anywhere. I make enough money for me and my family and I ain't going anywhere."

Sullenly, I glanced down at the counter, not sure how to respond. We were beyond the point of friendly conversation; I felt like a scolded child, embarrassed in a way that had more to do with the way I saw myself at that moment than the things he'd said, and suddenly I was struck with an odd and not entirely comforting thought: *Dad would really like this guy.*

Stan, having lost all interest in talking to me, picked his pencil back up and went back to work on his crossword. At that moment James walked back over with his hands in his pockets. "Let's just go," he said, glancing uneasily around the room as though the place had a bad smell.

"You're not getting anything?" I said.

He shrugged. "I can't decide. I guess this stuff doesn't really do it for me. And I'm, like, starving here."

"Yeah, but we've got twenty dollars."

He did this guilty go figure move with his head and then scratched the back of his neck. "It's just, I keep thinking about Dad, you know? Like, what would he say? It's weird. I'm thinking maybe we should just leave the stuff and go."

I could tell that something was bothering him about the situation, though I couldn't imagine what it was. This wasn't like my brother: why was James, of all people, worried about what Dad might have said? It didn't occur to me until later that maybe James felt that my having delegated this kind of job to him actually spoke way too clearly about the type of person I considered him to be. But I couldn't be sure then; all I knew was that it seemed self-defeating for us to leave empty-handed.

"This was your idea," I said. "The silver lining to a dark cloud and all that. We drove all the way—"

"Look Dave," he cut in sharply, "if you want to pick something out then go ahead. But if not, then let's just go because I'm exhausted and all I've had to eat today is a goddamn bagel."

But I didn't pick anything out. Instead, we thanked Stan, told him we were going to forfeit the store credit, suggested he give it to someone else. He raised a knobby hand, either in agreement or goodbye, we couldn't tell, keeping his basset hound's eyes on his booklet. "Somebody'll want them," he said as we made our way toward the door, meaning the magazines, the ones worth reselling. "I'm pretty sure about that."

††

By the time we left the store the air was beginning to cool

down and the first traces of evening gold had crept into the sky. It hadn't occurred to me how hungry I was until James had mentioned, and so when we spotted a diner a few miles up the road, I didn't bother asking before I pulled in. The warm, greasy aroma of sausage and bacon hit us as soon as we walked in the door. We slid into a booth by the window, a few seats down from a trio of old men who were laughing over a joke, their voices thin and brittle like old newspaper. The five of us were the only customers in the place. James lit a cigarette. "Steak and eggs, man," he said to himself, smiling, as he reached for one of the plastic menus tucked behind the napkin dispenser. "You better believe it."

I was still thinking about Stan back at the Tropic of Cancer, how he'd unloaded on me when I'd asked about the store. Some part of me was beginning to wish that we hadn't gotten rid of the magazines. It wasn't that I had any personal interest in them, but in light of the efforts Dad had taken to keep them hidden, it seemed maybe they had been something to hold onto. Obviously, they'd been important to him in one way or another, and as disconcerting as that may have been, I couldn't help feeling that they should have been important to us, too.

I considered running this by James, but when I looked up from my menu and saw the pained expression on his face, as though he were trying to lift something heavy, I dismissed it. His mouth was pursed into a thin whitish arc, and his brow was stiff and flat over his wide eyes.

"What is it?" I said. When he didn't respond, I followed his gaze to the counter behind us where a scrawny moon-faced waitress and a very large manager with a crew cut were whispering heatedly back and forth. Every few seconds the girl would glance over at us, fearful, and for a moment I was absurdly convinced that she had somehow pegged us as second-rate smut peddlers.

James turned to face the window, shaking his head. "Unfuckingbelievable," he muttered.

"What's going on?"

"That's her."

"Who?"

"Amelia." He nodded in the direction of the waitress. Again I craned my neck to get a good look at her. It took me a moment to place the name—Amelia, the girl who had accused James of trying to put his hand up her shirt at the space restaurant a year earlier.

"You're kidding," I said, but James just shook his head and sighed heavily.

As though somehow prompted by this realization, the manager appeared at our table. "Gentlemen," he said quietly, "I'm real sorry to do this, but I'm going to have to ask you to leave." He glanced back over his shoulder at the girl—Amelia—who was watching timidly from behind the counter, nibbling her fingernails. His sweaty blue business shirt was stretched taut over his enormous belly and chest.

"What for?" I said.

He cleared his throat and offered me an apologetic smile: *This wasn't my idea*, he seemed to be saying. Then he swiveled his head around to look at James, a move that seemed to require a great deal of effort. "Let's be civil about this, okay? I'm trying to keep the peace here."

James continued gazing out the window like a sulky child. I kept waiting for him to jump in with some punchy retort, but nothing came. Something had shut down inside of him. At some point I noticed that the table of old men had fallen silent and had turned their attention on us.

Taking a deep breath, I looked back at the waitress still cowering behind the counter, and then at the manager.

"My brother will have the steak and eggs and I'll have the double burger," I said.

The man's face stiffened as he braced his hands on the table and bent over toward me. "Fella," he responded, his low voice now fringed with impatience, "I'm asking nicely. Don't make me call the cops. We don't want to have to make a scene."

I leaned forward until my nose was only an inch or two from his. He didn't budge.

"Steak and eggs, double burger."

Well. I didn't know what the hell I was doing, but I could see from the way that Crew Cut's brow wrinkled up and his eyelids twitched that something unpleasant was about to go down, a scene I guess, and you know what's weird is that it actually excited me. What did I care about what had happened between my brother and that waitress? That had nothing to do with me. I was hungry and tired and had just spent my afternoon unloading my late father's secret stash of dirty magazines, and now here was this pit-stained ogre standing so close to me I could smell his shampoo, a man I imagined as one who deals with things in ways that require bulk and a flexible system of ethics, and would you believe that I was absolutely choking on exhilaration, I mean, totally fucking flying? It was as though the part of my brain that regulated self-preservation had malfunctioned.

The man cocked his head to speak, but before he could say anything James reached across the table and slapped my arm and then slid out of his seat, bumping not-so-accidentally into Crew Cut. "We're going," he declared.

"Good. Thank you," the man growled.

I looked up at my brother. He shook his head, a mitigating gesture. "We're going."

††

Outside in the parking lot James leaned against the truck and lit a cigarette; I didn't allow smoking inside the cab. I could see the manager watching us from the window of the restaurant, his thick arms crossed over his stomach. Behind him, the waitress hovered like a nervous wife. I was pretty worked up still, the way I used to get as a kid when James and I would wrestle on our bedroom floor. The matches had always ended the same way, with him pinning my head to the rug and me bawling, until around twelve years old when I was finally big enough to beat him, except by that point James wasn't interested in wrestling anymore.

"What the hell was that?" said James.

I smiled and shrugged. "He was a prick. I was hungry."

"That guy would have taken you apart, you know."

"I know."

"Well then."

We stood there in the dark parking lot until James had finished his cigarette, and then we climbed into the truck. As I started the engine I looked in the rearview and saw that Crew Cut was gone from the window.

"Hey," James said softly just as I was putting the truck into gear. My hand fell from the shift lever. "I never touched that girl."

"I know," I said, leaning away from him a little.

"I'm serious, Dave." Something in his gaze made me wince, a kind of hunger. "Not once. I swear to God."

I was quiet for some time. James and I had never really discussed the issue with the waitress, not in any real detail. There always seemed to be an unspoken understanding that my opinion on the matter was irrelevant.

Finally, I turned to look at him. "So, what do you want me to say?"

"I want you to say you believe me."

"Okay."

"Okay, you believe me, or just okay?"

"No, just—I don't know, James. I have to think about it."

"What the hell does that mean?" Now he twisted his entire body around in his seat to face me. "You have to think about it?"

"It's complicated, is what I'm saying."

"Complicated," he said as though he were spitting out a mouthful of sour milk.

I nodded. I was staring down at the back of my hand, still gripping the steering wheel.

"Okay, Dave. Look at me. Look at my face."

He leaned in toward me, placing his hand on the seat between us for support. I looked over at him. I was nervous, I didn't know why.

"Do you think I touched that chick, yes or no?" he said.

Outside, the three old men slouched out of the diner, their hands in their pockets and their shoulders hunched. I watched them amble off to their cars like animals slinking off to warm wooded dens to hibernate for the winter, and then I turned to James. "What the hell does it even matter what I think, anyway?" I said, trying to sound defiant but instead sounding like a petulant teenager.

He glared at me as if I had just smacked him in the face, a fierce, penetrating look that made something in me go scurrying for cover. It was like he didn't even recognize me. I didn't know how to explain it to him, how it wasn't an issue of believing or not believing him, because honestly, it's just never that simple with people like James, the margin of error is too big I guess you could say, and because of this I knew that whichever answer I gave wouldn't be entirely true.

"Fuck it," he said finally, turning back around and letting his head fall back against the seat with a soft thump. "Forget I asked."

For whatever reason, I thought about that day at the Jamaica Tavern, the girl in the red teddy sashaying past our table like an oncoming illness, and the look she'd given Dad, a kind of weary grimace, as though she regarded him as some kind of a threat. What was it she saw in him that the rest of us didn't? What had we missed?

"We should probably get back," I said. I didn't know who I was talking to, me or James. "Mom'll be home by now."

"Yeah, probably."

I put the truck into gear and circled around to exit the lot. As I prepared to pull out into the road, I looked over at the restaurant. Through the large windows, lit brightly from within, I could see the waitress, Amelia, perched sideways in one of the chairs at the counter with her head resting in her palm, a cigarette smoldering between two bony fingers, watching us warily as we pulled out into the road, as though we had stolen something from her.

Once the Queen is Gone

The idea was to drive to Louisiana overnight and show up at Petra's doorstep and tell her things about love and fulfillment and mistakes and forgiveness. Whether or not I actually meant any of these things, I couldn't say, but it didn't seem to matter; it was the spectacle I was going for. I had this image of her grabbing me by the collar and pulling me inside her apartment where we would whip off our clothes and work ourselves into a sweaty tangle right there on the floor.

It was just before noon when I crossed the Mississippi River into Baton Rouge. From the bridge, the city appeared as a modest assortment of hotels and office buildings nestled primly against the banks of the river. Petra's neighborhood was near the university, a few minutes south of the city proper, and was predominated by unassuming little apartment complexes with names like Cedar Creek and Pinecrest and, in her case, Oak Terrace.

"Oh, for God's sake," she said, scowling, when she answered the door.

I smiled nervously. "I brought you some taffy," I said, holding up the small pink box I had purchased at a truck stop in Chattanooga. It hadn't occurred to me until several hours into the trip that it might be in my best interest to show up with a gift. The woman working the counter had said that the taffy was handmade on a farm somewhere in Tennessee. I didn't know how Petra felt about taffy, but I figured she'd appreciate the idea of supporting a small business.

Petra crossed her arms and stepped out onto the small stoop. She was wearing jeans and a purple Louisiana State University sweatshirt. Her thick auburn hair was pinned into a haphazard bun on the back of her head. She didn't have on any makeup, and her complexion was wan and ashy. "Gabe, please tell me you didn't just drive all the way from Virginia for this."

"For what?"

"You tell me. What are you doing here?"

I looked down at the steps, the weathered LSU mat: *Go Tigers*!

"I had some vacation time," I blurted. It's a problem: when there's pressure, I lose my nerve.

She narrowed her eyes. "Vacation time?"

"Yeah, well, I mean, I didn't really have a plan or anything. I just wanted to go somewhere, you know? Get out of town for a while. Like New Orleans maybe, thought I'd do some gambling or something. But then I figured if I had come all this way to Louisiana, maybe I'd come see you."

She coughed heavily and ran a hand across her forehead. She didn't look too good; I wondered if maybe I'd woken her from a nap. "You have the worst fucking timing," she said. There was another coughing spasm, punctuated by a brief moan. "I'm sick and I have a midterm on Monday and I just wish you had called or something."

"I wanted it to be a surprise."

"Mission accomplished." She pointed to my duffel bag at my feet. "I take it you'll be staying here?"

I shrugged and shuffled uncomfortably. With Petra the trick was to appear as clueless as possible, like someone who needed her guidance. "Like I said, I didn't really have a plan. It's not a big deal. I mean, I can get a hotel room or something."

It was clear she wasn't buying it, but we both knew she wasn't going to turn me away. Petra's biggest handicap had always been her own good nature, the predictability of it. She got this from her parents, both of them history teachers, these nervous intellectual types, disarmingly kind, incapable of being rude.

After a moment she ushered me inside. The place was small and poorly lit and smelled vaguely of vanilla. There was a tattered leather armchair that I remembered from our old place in Richmond, a coffee table covered with textbooks, and a small TV situated precariously on a plant stand on the other side of the room. It was, I considered, the kind of place one might live in for a year or two while trying to figure some things out.

Petra was working toward a Ph.D. in biochemistry. She studied honeybees, or more specifically, their olfactory senses. The project she'd been working on for her dissertation involved introducing various synthetic pheromones into a colony and recording the changes in the bees' behavior. She'd tried to explain it to me over the phone one night shortly after she'd moved to Louisiana, how the colony is stratified by smell. "I mean, everything—reproduction, locating food sources, entry into the hive—it's all regulated by pheromones," she'd said with this crisp, scholarly inflection that I had found both endearing and a bit showy. "But when you start messing with those pheromones, it's like, *man.* The physiological changes are amazing. Sometimes they don't even recognize the queen anymore. The workers will stop providing for her. She might fly off to find another hive, but more often than not she just dies, which pretty much means the death of the whole colony. It's like, once the queen is gone, everyone is sort of screwed."

Now she took a seat on the futon sofa and plucked a cough drop out of a bag on the coffee table. "You've put on weight," she observed, placing the small white lozenge on her tongue.

"I quit smoking."

"Good for you."

"Thanks," I replied, trying to appear proud. This wasn't entirely true—I had tried nicotine patches for a while, but had quickly discovered that it's just more cost-effective to smoke—but I needed for Petra to believe that I had grown up in all the ways she never thought I would.

I was twenty-nine years old, but like most people that age, I felt much older. I was living in Richmond, Virginia, where I had spent the past six months working for a fencing company. I was at a point where things seemed to be happening way too fast for me to keep up. My body had begun to sag in unfortunate places. All of a sudden I had friends who were getting pregnant and joining book clubs and having tattoos removed. I would look around and think: did I miss something here?

And so now here I was in Petra's apartment, like she was supposed to somehow fix all this, like I'd never tried to convince myself that I would be better off without her.

Petra, looking to salvage a little civility from the situation, made some tea, and the two of us sat around the living room filling each other in on the past couple of years. I told her about my job with the fence company, how we'd recently put in eight hundred feet of electrical wire at the governor's mansion, and about our friends back in Richmond, which ones had gotten married, which ones were having kids, that kind of thing. Somehow I'd convinced myself that the two of us would instinctively fall back into our old familiar patterns of communication. But as we sat around her tiny living room trading our stories, I found myself growing more and more uncomfortable. It had been almost two years since we'd spoken face to face, and the conversation had a forced, hollow feeling to it, like we were on a blind date.

"How's school?" I said, sipping my tea.

Petra rolled her eyes and groaned. "Just put me out of my misery." She coughed into her fist.

"That bad, huh?"

"Well, maybe 'bad' isn't the right word. I mean, I like what I'm doing. Just busy, I guess. But like, super busy. Some days I'm lucky if I have time to pee."

I laughed a little. I'd heard this spiel before, back when we were living in Richmond. This was four years earlier, while she was trying to finish her bachelor's degree. We had a little un-air-conditioned apartment that overlooked the lacrosse field on the edge of campus. Everything was lovely and terrifying, thrumming with a sensual charge. At night we would lie together in our single armchair and watch sitcoms, and then we would crawl into bed and make love with the sort of self-indulgent recklessness that tends to define one's early twenties.

But this was precisely the problem, you see, the desperation of it all. What did we know? We were too young to appreciate the enormous weight of one another's needs, and so we argued frequently and often under the most ludicrous of pretexts—water on the bathroom floor, a jar of mayonnaise left out overnight. It was, I think, a way of punishing each other for our inability to live up to the other's expectations.

Then one day she announced that she was moving to Louisiana to pursue a doctorate, and I knew it was partly a test of my devotion: would I risk everything and go with her, or would I be practical and just stay there? Looking back, I'm pretty sure Petra had an inkling of which option I would pick, which was probably why she only nodded and grinned sadly when I told her I wasn't going.

There followed a period of dumb dry longing and late-night phone conversations, during which our voices would take on the same whispery lilt that in my mind seemed to characterize the very beginning of our relationship. I would ask her if she was seeing anyone and she would make this little sighing noise and say no, and she would ask me if I was seeing anyone, and I would also say no—a lie that I managed to rationalize on the grounds that she and I had vastly different interpretations for the word "seeing." And that's how it went for several months, until Petra, vexed by the sudden industry of encroaching adulthood, decided it would be in both our best interests to cease communication. "We're only fooling ourselves," she said over the phone one night. "It's just going to end with one of us getting hurt. Maybe both of us."

††

Later that afternoon Petra told me she had to go to the library for a while. "There's food in the fridge," she said, "and if you could take the trash out for me, that'd be super. I should be back in a few hours."

I felt like I should do something nice for her, so after she left I walked down to the ValuMart in the small Tudor-style strip mall at the end of her street to buy her some cold medicine. It was late October and the air was cool and dry and had a slight smoky odor to it. The gutters were choked with dead pine needles, small piles of them, swept hastily from the walkways of the drab brick apartment buildings.

At the store I grabbed a box of Comtrex from the pharmacy and got in line behind a young man who was struggling to unload items from his cart while wrangling with a couple of red-face little boys, both of whom I put at about four. I watched them scurry around the cart, chirping away in these high excited voices, pleading for candy, a toy, something. I was ready to go find another line to stand in when the father, who couldn't have been much older than me, crouched down and grabbed either kid by the arm and, clenching his teeth, hissed at them to be quiet and behave. His face was flushed, except for his mouth, which was stretched into a thin whitish arc, and in his voice I could hear the faint reedy strain of hysteria. I looked on with a disquieting sense of satisfaction as the boys' chubby little faces folded up like crumpled sheets of paper, and they began to wail. Deflated, the man let go of their arms and stood. He flashed me a look: *I didn't sign on for this.*

The whole scene registered with me in a weird way. There was a time when Petra and I had talked about having kids. We used to sit around our tiny apartment in Richmond, thinking up names for our unborn children. "I think we'll have good-looking kids," she once told me. I couldn't help wondering how she had arrived at this conclusion, though I didn't ask. Truth is, I never really wanted kids. It's just one of those things you talk about when you're young and want so badly to believe you're in love but know in the back of your mind that this isn't so. You can spot couples like this by the way they always keep an arm around one another's waist as if the wind might suddenly carry them away, how one might place his chin on the other's shoulder as they're scanning titles in the book store. That was Petra and me, and I can't say I hadn't missed it. There is a lot to be said for deluding one's self; the happiest people I've ever known have no idea how miserable they really are.

When the man had taken his bags and slumped off with his kids, I handed the medicine to the girl behind the counter. She gave me this conspiratorial half-smile and nodded toward the automated doors where the young father and his two boys had just exited. You could still hear the kids' wailing. "Poor guy," the girl said.

"Tell me about it," I replied. "Kids. I mean, Jesus."

"You got any?" She swiped the small box over the scanner.

"Me? Uh-uh. No way."

Sighing, she dropped the medicine into a plastic bag. "I am so getting my tubes tied," she said. Then, after a pause, "Do you have a ValuMart Plus card?"

††

Back at Petra's apartment I rifled through her kitchen drawers until I found an old spool of twine. I tied a rather sad-looking bow around the box of Comtrex and placed it on the cluttered table in the corner and then laid down for a nap. I woke up just before she returned from the library, sniveling and coughing miserably. "This guy kept shushing me," she said. "Every time I coughed, it was like, 'Shhh!' I wanted to punch him."

I watched her as she dropped her backpack on the table and spotted the box of Comtrex. She picked it up and turned to me, grinning. "You didn't have to do that."

"I didn't have a whole lot else going on."

"Well, thank you. That was sweet." She disappeared into the kitchen. Taking a seat on the futon, I grabbed a textbook entitled *Queen Rearing and Bee Breeding* from the scuffed-up coffee table in front of me and began to flip through it. I remembered the story Petra had told me years earlier about how her interest in bees had begun. She'd been mowing her back yard one afternoon when she was twelve. There was a small copse of shrubs in the far back corner near the fence that her father had never gotten around to cutting down, which made mowing in these areas somewhat tricky. "You basically had to run the mower up into the bushes," she'd explained to me. "It was the only way to get the grass. We didn't have a weed-eater." On the afternoon in question, however, she happened to have run over a small ground nest hidden at the base of one of the bushes. The bees were sucked up into the mower and then spit out of the exhaust, where they viscously descended upon her bare

113

legs, working their way up into her flimsy running shorts. Swatting blindly at the angry insects, she'd sprung over the small chainlink fence into her neighbor's back yard, where she tumbled into an above-ground swimming pool, one of these big round vinyl jobs. By the time she'd made it to a hospital, the swelling was so severe that the doctors had to cut her clothes off. They'd kept her there for nearly a week, pumping her full of cortisone and telling her over and over again how lucky she was not to be allergic.

When she had told me this story years earlier on one of our first dates, over a dinner of unremarkable Mexican food, I had been somewhat baffled by the note of sympathy in her voice, as though she actually felt sorry for the bees, and I couldn't help thinking of those tales you hear about kidnapped women who fall inexplicably in love with their captors.

"It was a respect thing, I guess, if that makes any sense," she'd said. "Just, you know, realizing what something is capable of. I mean, those little suckers were in my clothes and in my hair, just going totally nuts, this sort of, I don't know, collective conscious- ness, and it just blew me away how, when taken as a unit, these little things could do so much damage. It sounds weird, but if they hadn't landed me in the hospital, I probably wouldn't give a damn about bees."

††

That night I picked up some Chinese food from a place in the strip mall down the street. We sat around on Petra's sad little fu- ton, which had been designated as my bed, eating sweet and sour chicken and watching television. Her coughing had subsided a lit- tle, which I naturally attributed to the Comtrex, and thus secretly to me. The discomfort I'd felt earlier was mostly gone; in its place loomed a sort of breezy anticipation, sanctioned by the offhanded manner in which Petra's knee would brush against mine whenever she shifted positions.

"By the way," she said during a commercial, "sorry about ear- lier, the whole 'you've put on weight' thing. That wasn't very nice of me."

"It's not a big deal. I have gained weight."

"Yeah, but for a good reason, you know?"

After a while Petra went to take a shower. She emerged half an hour later, smelling sweet and clean and dressed in polka dotted pajama bottoms and a white t-shirt, and I felt my heart speed up just a little: there's something about a freshly-showered woman in her pajamas.

"I think I'm turning in," she said softly.

"Already?" It was barely nine o'clock.

"I'm exhausted. I think it's the medicine. Will you turn all the lights off before you go to bed?"

"Sure thing."

With a sleepy smile, she turned and headed into her bedroom. The door closed with an air of finality. I sat there staring at it for a few moments, as though I expected it to somehow vanish into the wall.

Stretching myself out on the futon, I took another piece of taffy from the box and flipped through the TV channels, thinking about Petra, fifteen feet away in the other room, nestled in the dark comfort of the bed we'd shared years earlier. I couldn't help feeling that I belonged in there with her, if only because that bed had played such an elemental role in our relationship. And from this line of thought sprang all these old memories of sex. Early morning romps with our shirts on. Petra's hair, damp with sweat, grazing my face and neck. The way she would nod her head and start panting *Yeah* when she was about to climax.

The point being, I guess, that there were things to consider, all this history, which was more or less the reason I was here, and which, consequently, made the idea of sleeping in separate rooms seem cold and unnatural and a little punitive.

I watched the last half of some gloomy cop drama and then crept to the bedroom door. Slowly and quietly, I peeked inside. Petra was already asleep; in all the time I'd lived with her, it had never taken more than five minutes from the time her head touched the pillow for her to doze off.

I eased my way into her bed, gently pressing my body against hers, savoring the smells of her shampoo and skin cream, intermixed with the slight sour odor of sleep. I took in the familiar topography of her face, the shadowy configurations of her cheeks and brow line, her long thin nose—Roman, she'd called it—and the tender curve of her ear. She was not an exceedingly beautiful girl, not someone who stood out in a crowd. But there was something about the way she carried herself that had always appealed to me, a practical elegance, like those women you see in fabric softener commercials.

I had positioned myself behind her so that my head was level with her back and so that, when I draped my arm over her body, prompting her to awaken with a quick jerk, her left elbow connected solidly with my upper lip. The pain was exquisite. Stifling a shriek, I covered my face and rolled away from her. I heard her murmur my name as I fell onto the floor, the slight rubbery taste of blood filling my mouth, not entirely unpleasant.

"Gabe, what the hell?" she said with a slight rasp in her voice, squinting down at me from the edge of the bed. "Christ, did I hit you?"

Through my hand, I mumbled, "Yes, you did."

Clumsily, I followed her to the bathroom, trailing small droplets of blood on the eggshell carpet. "I'll clean all this up," I sputtered—only the way I said it, it sounded like, "Uhkeenuhdissop."

"What did you say?"

I shook my head. *Forget it.*

She turned on the faucet and had me lean over the sink. Slowly, my focus came back to me, and I could see from Petra's expression that she wanted to ask me just what in the hell I was doing in her bed, but I knew she wouldn't, not just yet, not until the bleeding had stopped. And this was a good thing, because I didn't have an answer. I started thinking about the story she'd told me a couple years earlier, about the swarm of bees that had attacked her when she was a kid, and I wondered, with a kind of distant bewilderment, how it is that our passions tend to arise from the most damaging of instances.

She pressed a wet washcloth to my mouth, her smooth slender face only inches from mine, and I watched as the blood and water swirled together and trickled down the drain. Holding the bloody washcloth over my mouth, I looked up into the mirror and smiled at her. She smiled back in a way that reminded me of how she'd looked when I told her I wasn't coming to Louisiana with her, and then she did something incredible: taking my face in her hands like some delicate artifact, she angled my head downward and kissed me between my eyebrows. Her lips lingered there for a few seconds, and I felt her hair brush lightly against my chin.

My first inclination, naturally, was to return it. But when she let go and stepped back, I realized that it was actually nothing more than a consolation gift. I could see it in her face, in the long, mournful pressure of her gaze: this was the only thing she had left to offer me, this pitiful little peck on the forehead, and suddenly I began to feel as though I had lost something priceless.

She flitted into the kitchen and returned moments later with a Baggie full of ice. "Here," she said, taking the washcloth from me and carefully placing the Baggie on my swollen nose. I winced. After a minute or so she said, "How is it now?"

I tried to smile, which only amplified the dull throbbing. "A little better," I replied.

"Is it broken, you think?"

"No, I think it'll be okay."

When we'd finally gotten the bleeding under control, we shuffled out into the living room and turned on the TV. I told Petra she should go back to bed, that she needed her rest if she was going to get better, but she just shrugged and said she was too wired up, all that blood. We sat there for a while watching some old black and white gangster film, laughing at the hokey dialogue. We didn't speak; to do so, it seemed, would be to jeopardize some fragile understanding that I wanted to sustain as long as possible, at least until I'd made it back home, out of Petra's life.

For now, though, we had the television, and we had the taffy, which Petra picked through steadily until pretty soon the box was empty and she had fallen asleep with her head cocked to one side, resting awkwardly against my shoulder, and I knew this was going to do a number on her thin little neck, but I still couldn't bring myself to wake her, not just yet.

The Cosmic Brethren

1.

The Budget Lodge outside of Fairfield, Virginia, is one of these long, flat, side-of-the-road places that most people would pass over in favor of something more recognizable, a Holiday Inn maybe, or a Best Western. But as Walter has already pointed out, we don't want recognizable; we want someplace unassuming and quiet and largely overlooked by travelers. The front office is little more than a small booth with a metal transaction drawer and a grimy Plexiglass window, at the top of which the words NO CHECKS have been spelled out in thick blocky lettering with what appears to be electrical tape. There's a broken Pepsi machine positioned nearby, at least fifteen years old, judging from the logo, which has faded from red and blue to a sickly-looking yellow and green. When I checked in earlier today, the clerk—a heavyset Hispanic man with a shaved head and a Tweety Bird tattoo on his forearm—looked me over suspiciously when I asked for a room as far away from the road as possible. "Because of all the traffic noise," I said, gesturing dismissively in the direction of the road. I couldn't tell him, of course, that the reason for this was to minimize the risk of anyone who happened to be driving by noticing me and my ex-wife Ellen smuggling our twenty-year-old daughter Julie into our room like a hostage. Which, technically speaking, she is.

We've just returned from the Cosmic Brethren compound a few miles down the road, me and Ellen and Walter, our intervention specialist, where we snatched Julie out of the surrounding peach orchard while she was out picking peaches. The compound itself is nothing more than a collection of cheap plywood shacks built around a pre-existing farmhouse at the bottom of a large land basin. It was purchased years ago with the combined savings of the first members, along with the orchard, which surrounds the house on three sides. The long rows of peach trees stretch up the long sloping sides of the basin, toward the curtain of pines insulating the property from the nearby highway.

We parked my station wagon off to the side of a small gravel trail that cut through the trees to a red clay service road running the perimeter of the property, which provided us with a solid panoramic view of the area while giving us plenty of cover from the Brethren far below, who were scattered throughout the vast orchard, steadily working their ways down the rows of peach trees, dragging behind them large baskets full of the plump pinkish fruit.

"Which one is she?" said Walter, sitting in the back seat of the car. He was wearing khaki slacks and a button-down shirt the color of mouthwash.

"Not sure," I said, straining forward from behind the steering wheel. From where we sat, it was impossible to tell them apart. In their off-white hand-woven tunics, the tiny figures appeared as an assemblage of bored-looking ghosts. They were spaced far enough apart in the orchard that they wouldn't have been able to speak to one another without shouting. Not that they even bothered; they went about their business as stony-faced and mechanically as a prison chain gang. For a moment, I considered that maybe they were on something, a sedative of some sort—something to keep them docile, obedient. But then I remembered that the Brethren opposed drugs of any kind, even caffeine. Such toxins, as they referred to them, were one of the major contributors to the mind's inability to experience true peace.

"There she is, right there," Ellen gasped, stabbing at the window with her pointer finger. "You see her?

I leaned over and craned my neck to get a good look out the passenger's window. There was Julie, about forty yards out, standing on her tiptoes to paw through the thick boughs of leaves on one of the trees in search of fruit.

Walter and I eased out of the car, leaving our doors open; the sound of them closing would have been loud enough for the Brethren to hear. We crept down the small gravel path and then across the service road, over the small ridge, and then we hid behind the peach trees at the orchard's edge. Crouched in the stiff, wiry scrub, I thought of the neighborhood-wide games of Capture the Flag my brothers and I used to play when I was a kid. Nothing was off limits in terms of hiding places back then; we'd crawl on our bellies through scummy drainage ditches, scale back fences and hunker down in dark, musty tool sheds. The act of hiding, I considered, must be the basis for at least ninety percent of all children's games.

Julie was a few rows over from us and had her back turned. Walter glanced over at me and arched his eyebrows as if to ask if I was ready. I nodded once—not because I was ready but because I knew that it was impossible to ever truly be ready for something like this—and then the two of us darted out and grabbed Julie by the arms. It was immediately clear that she'd lost a good bit of weight since the last time I'd seen her, which made it easy for us to wrestle her to the ground, and her skin was the color of skim milk; all of this, I knew, was the result of the sensory deprivation pods. Walter had shown me a photo a few days earlier: a large capsule-shaped coffin, the insides lined with black felt cushioning, the purpose of which is to simulate the physical and emotional rigors of deep space travel. The Brethren spend a minimum of four hours a day in them in order to acclimate themselves to the cruel darkness.

From his pocket, Walter produced a white plasticuff, the kind they use on those real-life cop shows, which, after some difficulty, he managed to slip around Julie's wrists and then tighten with a single jerk on the end.

"What are you doing?" I said as I struggled to keep Julie still, to which Walter only threw me an impatient glance.

Julie screamed out for help as we dragged her back through the trees, her voice shrill as a car alarm and raspy with panic, though fortunately the rest of the Brethren, alerted by the sound of her cries, were too far away to make it to the top of the hill before Walter and I reached the station wagon. Ellen, waiting anxiously outside the car, ran around to the back to open the door. "Why is she tied up?" she said as Walter and I laid Julie down inside on the stained brown floorboard, but again Walter didn't answer. He gathered up Julie's legs and folded them into the car. Ellen climbed inside and lay down next to her, trying to calm her down. Walter and I raced around and leapt into the car, and then the four of us took off down the service road in a cloud of orange dust, just as a couple of tunic-clad young men reached the top of the hill behind us.

Now, having returned to the motel, I back the station wagon up to the room, alongside Walter's black Acura, until the rear tires hit the curb, and then Ellen and I run around to the back of the car and heft Julie out. The last bit of daylight is fading over the trees behind the building; the lights at the edge of the parking lot have already come on. I've got my arms hooked through Julie's from behind, and Ellen's got her feet, though with Julie bucking and wriggling so much, it's hard to keep hold as we lug her inside. She smells like grass clippings and sweat. The room is small with salmon-colored walls and brown water stains on the ancient ceiling panels. There's a single queen-sized bed in the center and a small table-and-chair set off to the side. The cracked porcelain sink in the back of the room is covered almost entirely by a fine layer of orange rust, as are the faucet and spigots and the inside of the toilet bowl. As soon as we make it through the door my hands slip from beneath Julie's arms, and down she goes, onto her back, thunking her head on the maroon-pattered carpet. I can hear the wind go out of her in a single abrupt gasp, and I feel the spot in my brain that, in a textbook illustration, would say *Mortified* or *Dread*, light up like a pinball machine as she coughs soundlessly.

Ellen, slapping her hands over her mouth, kneels down beside her. "Oh, Honey," she whines. "Oh Honey, oh god." I hunker down next to Julie's head. All kinds of little alarms are going off inside me. The fall couldn't have been more than maybe two feet, but

I mean, this is my kid here, and we actually fucking *dropped* her, and of course I'm wondering for the millionth time how it is that people like me are even allowed to bring children into the world in the first place. It's a question I've been asking myself over and over for the past twelve years, ever since Ellen and I split up.

"Sweetie, you okay?" I say, trying not to sound too panicked. The fall only seems to point to the larger, now-glaring fear that maybe this wasn't such a terrific idea, this intervention, that if something were to go wrong, we could end up pushing her even farther away. And obviously this is a poor start.

Julie blinks heavily a few times and coughs once more and then fixes us with a look of such raw hatred that I feel something in me curdle. Her eyes are narrowed into slits, her lips pursed. I'm actually a little relieved that her hands are tied.

Is this really my daughter?

Ellen, panting—either from the effort of carrying Julie inside or from the emotional drain of it or, more likely, both—reaches out to stroke Julie's greasy, dirty-smelling hair, but Julie jerks her head away. "We only want to help you, sweetie," Ellen coos, which is of course a hundred percent true, but is also probably the lamest thing she could say right now, because obviously Julie expects to hear this kind of stuff, these feathery reassurances. Part of the Brethrens' indoctrination process involves spending a lot of time deconstructing such statements in order to demonstrate their emptiness—"for your own benefit", "a danger to yourself", etc.— and so naturally anything we say right now is only going to reinforce her skepticism.

Walter, who's been standing over near the TV this whole time watching us like a director observing a troupe of blindingly un-skilled actors rehearse a scene, hunkers down and tells me to help him roll Julie onto her side so that he can cut the binding off. Once he's snipped it with a small red pocket knife, Julie twists away from us and scrambles across the floor on her hands and knees like a frightened animal, into the small narrow alcove between the bed and the far wall, where she curls herself up into a ball, clutching her knees to her chest.

Ellen and I move toward her, but Walter stops us. "Just give her some space, let her calm down," he says as he walks to the sink at the back of the room to wash his hands.

Reluctantly, I sit down on the edge of the bed, and all at once it hits me how exhausted I am. I spent most of last night lying awake in my fusty motel room wondering how in the hell we all got to this point, me and Ellen and Julie; you rent out of a couple of rooms in some fleabag motel in Southwestern Virginia for the purpose of staging an intervention for your daughter, who happens to be a member of an obscure UFO cult—and naturally you find yourself retracing your steps.

Ellen and I were married for just over ten years before we divorced in 1997. She's a small woman, *petite* I guess you would say, with tiny, delicate features and thick strawberry-blonde hair. She's an engineer for the city of Roanoke, one of the only women to have ever held the position, and because of this she's cultivated this defensive air over the years. Julie lived with Ellen up until she moved in with the rest of the Brethren a year ago. She used to spend the weekends with me in Salem—a twenty-minute drive from her mother's place—sometimes birthdays and holidays too, and with each visit it seemed as if we recognized each other a bit less, that we were steadily becoming strangers to one another. She looks like a slightly shorter version of her mother, with the exception of her long rounded nose, which she inherited from me, along with her oversized ears and the field of ginger-colored freckles beneath her eyes. I've often wondered had I been around more when she was growing up, whether she would bear less of a resemblance to her mother. I'm a senior sales rep for a small but profitable medical supply company—bone screws, cardiac valves, etc.—a job that for the past twenty years has kept me on the road for considerable periods of time, and I'm not so clueless as to overlook the possibility that this might have had something to do with our current situation, my prolonged absences, I mean, though, to be fair, it's just a job, after all, a means of providing for myself and my family, and the fact is I'm pretty good at it, always have been. A good salesman needs to be able to understand people's motivations, the engines that power their needs. You have to know what they want when they don't even know. And after twenty years in the business, I think I've developed quite a talent for this.

All of which once again begs the question: How did we end

up here?

**

The deprogramming is scheduled to begin tomorrow, only Walter says not to call it deprogramming. Too loaded with unpleasant connotations, he says. "'Strategic thought reformation' is what I call it," he told us on the phone a few months back when we contacted him about helping us to stage an intervention with Julie who, for a year now, has been a member of the Cosmic Brethren, living in their compound on the hilly outskirts of Lexington, Virginia. Walter estimates that the process should take about four days—an overzealous estimation in my opinion, but when I pointed this out to him he was quick to rebut. "Really, it's just that people are shockingly uncomplicated," he said. "Getting in there, into her head, is the tricky part, but once I do, it's smooth sailing from there."

Right now, however, we just need sleep, all four of us. We've booked three rooms, side by side; Julie's in the middle room. Because Walter says it's a not great idea to leave Julie alone in a room for long stretches of time—*flight risk* was how he classified her—and because the thought of the four of us sharing the same motel room for the next four days seemed like a terrific way to sabotage the intervention altogether, Ellen and I came up with a plan for us to trade off nights sleeping in Julie's room. The other two of us will take the rooms on either side (Walter's already laid claim to the one on the left, I think because it's closer to the vending machines). Not surprisingly, Ellen has already volunteered for tonight, and I admit that I am more than a little relieved; at this point I'm mildly terrified to be alone with my daughter.

Once we've all managed to collect ourselves, Walter and Ellen and I shuffle outside onto the small walkway outside the building. We stay near the window so we can keep an eye on Julie, still curled up between the bed and the wall, the small yellowish mound of the top of her head rising a few inches above the bedspread. Night has settled in already; there's the watery trill of crickets coming from the overgrown shrubbery running along the edge of the parking lot, and all at once I feel like I'm light years from home. It's a feeling

I've experienced countless times in the past in questionable motels along my sales routes, but this time it's different, more defined.

"You two did really well today," Walter says. "For you, this is probably the hardest part. You should be really proud of yourselves."

He's trying to keep our spirits up, like a parent talking to a child whose Little League team has just lost. It's a condescending doctor tactic, although I know that Walter doesn't mean it this way. Nonetheless I have to work hard to stifle a smirk when Ellen turns around and looks up at him and says icily: "You never said anything about tying her up."

"No, I most certainly did not," Walter replies. "Do you know why? Because it would have jeopardized our goals for this thing."

Now Ellen and I are staring at the man as if he's just sprouted a second head, and it's a testament to his persuasive abilities that I actually want to hear him out.

"Look," he says, "I told you from the beginning that you were going to have to trust me, that you might not like some of my methods, but that they're for the best. Didn't I say that?"

We nod, me and Ellen, even though it's a rhetorical question.

He continues, somewhat quieter: "I can understand your reservations. Really, I can. But we're not going to get through this thing if you don't trust me. I can't run every single thing by you, know what I mean? If you want this thing done right, you have to let me work. We got her here, didn't we?"

No doubt this is a speech he's given countless times in the past in one form or another. That's how it is with Walter, I've learned: everything that comes out of his mouth seems like a carbon copy of something that's already been said.

When he's gone, Ellen turns back to me and rolls her eyes. "'This whole thing.' Did you hear him?"

"Yeah."

"Cocky prick."

"It's what we're paying him for. He's right."

She nods and falls silent, though I can tell she's still aggravated. Out in the distance, cars slip past in the night. Ellen gazes dolefully at the motel. "My poor baby," she mumbles, hugging herself against the evening chill. "My little girl."

"That farm looked nice," I say.

She turns to me. "What the hell is that supposed to mean?"

"Nothing. I'm just saying. It was a pretty piece of land."

"You could barely even see it, Lee. It was too far off."

"I could see it. It wasn't that far."

Ellen turns away and looks out across the parking lot. I really do feel bad for her. I know that everything I'm saying is probably the exact opposite of what I should be saying, but I'm trying to maintain a sense of rationale here, meaning that I don't want to let my emotions get the better of me, which, as Walter states in his book—*Free At Last: Exit Strategies for Victims of Spiritual Abuse*, by Walter Shapiro, Ph.D.—is the easiest way to derail an intervention before it's even begun (Chapter 2, "Preparations"). That's the only way we're going to make it through this thing, by keeping our cool. I meant what I said: the farm really was pretty.

Thing is, I know Ellen's probably blaming herself for this whole mess, scouring her memory for anything that, in theory at least, could have had some bearing down the line on her daughter's psychological state—dropping acid in college, or not getting enough vitamin C. And while I want to tell her that she should go easy on herself, that there's no way to anticipate this stuff, that there are kids out there right now with semiautomatic weapons and crack-addicted babies, I know that the trick with Ellen is to just stay quiet and let her be upset, and so now, standing outside the motel room door, listening to the low, sad thrum of traffic on the highway in the distance, that's exactly what I do. I keep my mouth shut, until finally she sighs heavily, as though the breath has been building in her for some time, and she says, "Okay, I'm heading in. I'm exhausted."

"Night," I say, maybe with a bit too much enthusiasm. She forces a smile and then disappears inside the room, closing the door behind her. Interesting how neither of us so much as mentioned the intervention tomorrow.

2.

Most of what I know about the Cosmic Brethren comes from the Rubbermaid tub full of information—pamphlets and photographs and such—that Walter brought along to his first meeting with Ellen and me at Ellen's house and which he's now brought along to the motel. It was in 1987 that Owen Grubb, a technician at a waste water treatment facility just south of Lexington, claimed to have been contacted one evening by members of a race of godlike beings whom he later referred to as the Zetas (it was said the term "Zetas" was implemented for purposes of brevity, as the species' actual name comprised over three-thousand syllables). According to the file, Grubb, who had been hospitalized some years prior for bipolar disorder (there's a photocopy of a hospital discharge report in the tub; I don't think to ask Walter how he obtained it), claimed to have been abducted during his sleep and taken on board a massive vessel that "looked to be made almost entirely out of light." The Zetas—who were somewhat humanoid in appearance, with the exception of their elongated limbs and translucent skin that seemed to glow from within, much like the ship itself—explained telepathically to Grubb that they had been studying Earth for some time, observing the curious emergence and disappearance of various civilizations like so many blips on a radar screen. The human race, they said, was doomed, destined to be obliterated by its own selfish devices.

However, the Zetas had cultivated a planet—referred to tentatively as "New Earth," again to accommodate humans' linguistic handicaps—in the Andromeda galaxy specifically for those humans they deemed worthy. It was only here, on this new planet, that the human soul could be released from its bodily prison in order to experience true harmony. There had been other folks like Grubb, emissaries of sorts, men and women who, over the course of centuries, had been contacted by the Zetas to impart upon mankind their message of peace and love as a means of obtaining transcendental wisdom—Jesus and Muhammad being some of the more notable ones.

The creatures entrusted Grubb with the task of recruiting a group of suitable individuals to be transported to New Earth, where the Zetas would bestow upon the Brethren their secret of eternal life and everlasting peace. Presently, there are forty-two members of the group, including Julie: twenty-two males and twenty females, most of them college dropouts like her or burnt-out white collar drones slogging through a midlife crisis that's gotten severely out of hand. This includes Grubb, who stayed in the main bedroom of the farm until, it is said, his need for privacy led to the construction of a small two-bed-two-bath house a half mile down the road. The members sleep about five to a room, in hand-made bunks. A suspiciously large number of them come from IT backgrounds, and so they support the group by hiring themselves out as web designers to some of the smaller companies in the area. Then, during the summer months, there are the peaches, which they sell at local farmer's markets and to a handful of higher-end restaurants in the region.

**

In the morning, I head over to the small diner next to the motel to have a cup of coffee before things get under way and to pick up some breakfast for the four of us (Walter vetoed Ellen's proposal that we go eat at the diner, claiming that the success of the intervention depended largely upon our ability to keep Julie sequestered, insulated from distraction). A tepid wind stirs the trees behind the motel and on the other side of the road; this afternoon will be a scorcher, and then later this week, rain. The diner is long and narrow like a train car. A seafoam green counter runs most of the length of one wall, and the other wall is lined with brown vinyl booths, tattered and stained from countless years of grease and smoke and bodies, as are the once-white floor tiles, which have taken on the sickly coloration of poorly-tended teeth. I've always had an affinity for places like this. When I was growing up, my father drove a bus for the city, and there was a small greasy spoon near our house where he would go every morning before work for a cup of coffee and maybe a plate of eggs. Sometimes during the summers and holidays when I wasn't in school, he'd let me tag along. We'd sit at the grimy counter, him with his coffee and me with my orange juice, like two men attempting to collect themselves before their workday began. I don't think we ever said more than a few words to each other during these times, though looking back, I'm pretty sure that was what made those mornings so great: it's good to be able to just sit with your father, to not feel pressured to talk, to let the silence do all the work.

Now I take a seat on one of the stools at the counter. The waitress, a squat elderly woman with drab grey curls and a spotty complexion, waddles over to me.

"How you doing?" she says with a pointed lack of interest.

"Getting by, I suppose."

"That's all you can really ask for. Coffee?"

"Yes, please. Can I order some breakfast to go?"

"That's fine."

I wait for her to produce a pencil or a pad of paper, but she just stands there, hands braced against the counter, looking at me like I'm a Christmas gift she plans to return. "It's a pretty sizeable order," I say.

"Meaning what?"

I order four orders of scrambled eggs, hashbrowns, and toast, and two coffees for Ellen and Walter. The woman turns and, in a little sing-song kind of shorthand, calls out the order to the two cooks standing behind the heat lamps: "Four order scrambled, hash-toast four times!" She turns back to me. "Anything else?"

"Actually, do you have any fruit?" Julie doesn't eat meat.

"Oranges. Though we usually just cut those up for garnish and whatnot."

"That'll work. Could I get a couple oranges?"

She nods, satisfied. "And we got some cantaloupe too, if you want it. Food'll be up in a bit."

Back in the motel room, Ellen and Walter and I dig into our meals, while Julie, still cowering in the far corner between the bed and the wall—she spent the night there, despite Ellen's pleas that she sleep in the bed—begrudgingly nibbles the orange slices. No one talks. There seems to be an unspoken agreement not to mention what happened last night or what's about to happen. Why is this? Hard to say; maybe we just want to enjoy the last little bit of silence before the intervention starts up and things get heavy. We all focus on our meals, cramming forkfuls of goopy eggs and wads of buttery toast into our mouths.

Once we've finished eating, Walter, dressed in the same business shirt and slacks as yesterday, tells me and Ellen that it's time to get started. He pulls up one of the railback chairs to the small alley between the bed and the wall. "Julie," he says softly, cautiously, "do you know why you're here?"

Julie looks us over with a contemptuous scowl. There's a wet sliver of orange pulp on her bottom lip by the corner of her mouth. My instinct is to reach down and wipe it off; I'm guessing Ellen is thinking the same thing.

"I know why you think I'm here," she says, her voice as arid and lifeless as the surface of Mars.

"Okay, why's that?"

"Because you don't believe in our mission. You don't believe in the Ascent." The Ascent is the name given to the process by which humans are selected and groomed for travel to New Earth.

"Do you think we should believe in it?" says Walter.

Julie closes her eyes and shakes her head. "Nobody ever asked you to, that's your whole problem. We live our lives in accordance with the One Truth, but we've never asked for acquiescence from anyone." It's a line from the Cosmic Brethren Mission Statement, word-for-word. I recognize it from the website.

"Is that why you think we brought you here," says Walter, "because we don't agree with your beliefs?"

Julie fixes him with a steely gaze. "You kidnapped me, okay? I didn't demand that you believe what I believe." She's talking to all three of us now. "You're not ready for it. I understood that. I left it alone. I didn't sneak up in the night and grab you and throw you in a car."

Walter's nodding at all this and stroking his chin as though he's contemplating a chess move. His trim jaw is covered in a thin layer of brownish fuzz this morning—why bother shaving, under the circumstances?—though it doesn't make him look slovenly or unkempt; rather, it seems to give him an air of rugged integrity. I find this both enviable and annoying. He says to Julie: "I—we, I mean, can certainly appreciate why you're upset. Honestly. What I was hoping here, Julie, is that if we try to understand your position better, maybe you would try to understand ours. What do you think?"

"My position," she scoffs. "You're not interested in my position. Stop lying to yourselves. You're afraid of my position. You're afraid that once you've seen the Light of the Zetas, you're going to start questioning your own beliefs, your own systems of thought, because you know deep down that your heart is a reservoir of doubt. You're afraid of love. It terrifies you." At some point I notice that my mouth is hanging open and I'm clutching my knees, as though I'm at that part in the movie where I'm about to find out who the killer is. It's horrifying how unlike herself she sounds, and yet at the same time I'm actually a little thrilled by the story itself, the absurd scope of it. She says, "As for your position, I mean, I've been there. I've done it. I left it behind. I found real love because I realized that my body doesn't own my soul. I have been freed by the Light of the Zetas."

"But what about your parents?" Walter asks, motioning to Ellen and me. "You don't think they love you?"

There's a flicker of something across her face, sorrow maybe, or disappointment. "They think they do. It's not their fault. But a soul bound by flesh cannot truly know love, because love lives outside the body."

"We do love you, Honey. You might not believe it, but we love you so much." Ellen chimes in. Walter throws her an agitated glance and then, catching himself, looks back at Julie. I can tell from the tiny tremor in my ex wife's voice that she's probably inches from tears, and the sound of it makes me feel as if someone has just yanked a drawstring at the back of my head, pulling the skin taut. Partly it's because I don't do well around crying people, but also because I know how much Ellen hates for people to see her cry. Even back during the last few years of our marriage, when we could hardly go a day without a fight, she almost never cried, and when she did she would scurry into the bathroom so that I couldn't see her, always returning moments later with pink puffy rings around her eyes and a new sense of composure.

Sitting back in his chair with his legs crossed and his hands clasped on his knee—a look of striking repose—Walter asks Julie to tell him about how she became a member of the Cosmic Brethren. His approach, as he's explained to Ellen and me, is non-confrontational: he prefers to ask large open-ended questions and then use the subject's own responses to demonstrate the logical inconsistencies in their reasoning. Julie continues to glare at him silently for a moment and Walter endures it with the cool disposition of a Zen monk, before finally it becomes clear to her that the only way out of this is to just play along, at least for a little while. And so, in a sulky murmur, she tells Walter the same story she told me two years earlier, shortly before dropping out of school in Lexington.

She had taken a weekend trip into Charlottesville with some friends to participate in an antiwar rally. Julie has always had a hard time maintaining emotional distance from the things she's passionate about; back in high school she classified herself to Ellen and me as a progressive liberal and then later as a neo-socialist, and I couldn't help but wonder if she knew what these titles meant or if she just liked their ring of intellectualism. In college, she insisted on buying her groceries at co-ops and farmers' markets, and during her sophomore year of college, she had lobbied (unsuccessfully) for the Board of Visitors to discontinue the sale of all university apparel, claiming that the garments were manufactured in Malaysian sweatshops. The antiwar protest in question had taken place on the University of Virginia campus. Really it was nothing more than a few hundred hoodie-clad college liberals hoisting signs and chanting while a handful of cross-armed cops and school officials looked on from a safe distance, bored. Julie and her friends had hoped that the protest might draw some of the local media, but as it was, there were only two camera crews there—WLDG in Charlottesville, who actually spent most of their time chatting with the underwhelmed cops, and a student news crew from the university.

After the less-than-stellar protest, Julie and her friends had wandered into the quaint downtown arena of pubs and coffee shops to find some lunch. They were despondent and irritated with themselves for their apparent failure to generate the kind of support they had hoped. While making their way down one of the small restaurant strips, they were approached by two young men in tattered jeans and frayed flannels—backpackers, Julie had assumed from the large packs they carried on the backs of their pallid, tawny frames. The area was a well-known pit stop for folks hiking the Appalachian Trail. The boys stopped the group of young people, not impolitely, and, after brief introductions, one of them said: "What does it mean to you to be truly at peace with yourselves?"

Assuming the boys to be evangelicals, Julie's friends excused themselves and walked on, but Julie, guileless to a fault, remained behind to hear what they had to say. By her rationale, she owed it to these two boys to hear them out, if only because they were all three joined by a very poignant sense of conviction, as evidenced by the small leaflet they gave her—*THERE IS MORE TO THE UNIVERSE THAN YOU CAN IMAGINE!!!* printed in bright lettering across the top—before the three of them ducked into a nearby café to talk.

By the time Julie described the scene to me months later during her yearly Father's Day visit to my apartment in Salem, she had already dropped out of school; in another few months she'd donate her car and most of her clothes to the local Goodwill, a move that would send me into loud spasms of fury, mostly from the realization that I was helpless to do anything about it.

But that was all to come later; at that point, neither Ellen nor I were entirely sure what we should do. We talked about it on the phone regularly. Both of us wanted to believe that it was some kind of rebellion, a phase that Julie would eventually grow out of. It wasn't the loss of a college degree that bothered us the most—though that was certainly part of it—but more that she seemed determined to jettison every ounce of potential she had. She was the brightest, most driven individual I'd ever known, and now here she was, selling off all her belongings so that she could move into a ramshackle farmhouse to sell peaches. Even now, sitting here in the small motel room next to Ellen and the frighteningly well-composed Walter Shapiro, it's a struggle for me not to grab my daughter by her thin shoulders and shake her back and forth and howl into her face: *You are smarter than this! You had a 3.9 GPA! You were going to go to law school!*

**

The morning wears on, a litany of broad, open-ended questions. What is it like on the farm? How well does she get along with the other Brethren? What is it about the promise of immortality that she finds so compelling? Of course Walter, having spent the better part of a decade writing about groups like the Brethren, probably knows more about them than the Brethren themselves; I have to keep reminding myself that the questions are for Julie's benefit, not ours. Forcing her to think them over and then articulate her responses allows her to see for herself the flimsiness of her logic (as spelled out in Chapter 1 of *Free at Last*, "The Five Precepts of Strategic Thought Reformation").

Walter asks Julie if she's at all apprehensive about the long journey through uncharted space to the Zetas' home planet. "It's not uncharted," Julie replies irritably. "The Zetas were making the trip before human beings had even evolved."

He nods gravely. "You're right. I'm thinking too narrowly. It's just a long trip, is all, you know? I mean, long-long." He flashes her a sly grin. "I'm wondering how you're going to hold up."

Julie narrows her eyes. "We've made adequate preparations."

"The pods?"

"Among other things."

**

There's truth to the notion that mental work is more grueling than physical work, because by noon, after nearly five hours of sitting in the same spot and talking only every minute or so, my head is too foggy to form anything close to a complete thought. I feel the same way I used to back in college after spending a week cramming for finals. I can see that Ellen is worn out, too; it's in the pouchy folds of her face and the way her body sags like an unused puppet. Julie's still in the corner, holding her knees to her chest, though all of the emotion appears to have drained from her face, leaving her with a blank, grayish affect. Under the circumstances, this qualifies as progress.

Around twelve-thirty, Walter calls a stop for the day, and it's like someone opening a pressure valve somewhere in the room, the way we all seem to sink down with relief. Ellen, clearly eager for a break from the motel room, offers to pick up a couple pizzas from a place we passed on the way to the motel. "Julie, Hon," I say, "you want to step outside, get some fresh air?" But she doesn't say anything.

"Let's just give her some space for a bit," Walter says to me softly, and so he and I head outside, where the steamy summer heat hits me like a fist. We've only been inside a few hours, but you would think I've been living underground for the past decade. Shading our eyes with our hands, we wander out into the mostly empty parking lot.

"Think she'll be okay in there?" I say.

He glances toward the room and nods. "So long as we don't wander too far. There's really nowhere for her to go, anyway."

"How do you think it's going?"

He bobs his head thoughtfully, making the wings of his hair sway. "Pretty well, I think. She's wearing down a little. By tomorrow she'll be like clay." This last part he emphasizes with a thin conspiratorial smile, and I notice that the genial tone he used with Julie is gone, replaced by the kind of humorless affect you might expect from someone who, like Zetas, has pretty much given up on most of mankind. I don't know why I'm not more bothered by this.

"So," I say to Walter, "are these things usually this intense?"

He laughs. "You kidding? This is nothing. You can't imagine the things I've had to deal with. Look at this." Pushing up his sleeve, he holds his hand out, palm upward. "See those marks around the thumb?"

Squinting, I examine his slender hand until I spot the two arcs of pink scar tissue at the base of this thumb. "Yeah, I see them."

"A girl did that, you believe it? Years ago. About as old as Julie. She was from the Unarious Academy of Science. You've heard of them? Interesting group, a lot like the Brethren. Not many left at this point, though. We were at her folks' house, me and the mom and dad and the brother and the grandma. Grandma was a Jehovah's Witness, and she kept singing these hymns—'Onward, Christian Soldiers,' that kind of thing—over and over again."

I chuckle lightly; it seems expected. Across the parking lot, a dusty red pickup swings into a space, coughing up clouds of gray exhaust. A heavy man in a white t-shirt climbs out and lugs two large duffel bags out of the back. With his head down, he carries them to his door, as though he's marching toward a jail cell. He glances over at Walter and me before disappearing into his room.

Walter continues: "So, this thing goes on for two or three days, it's easy to lose track. And it's all pretty standard, I suppose: she cries, the parents cry, the brother cries, and after a while everything seems to be on the up and up. The girl—the client—seems to be coming around.

"Well, at one point she's sitting in this armchair in the living room, and it looks like she's close to the Acceptance phase. And so I lean down and put my hand on her shoulder. Trying to be comforting, you know? Then, out of nowhere, she jerks around, real quick, like a snake"—he twists his upper body to demonstrate—"and she bites me, hard. She's got her teeth in the meat of my hand and she won't let go. Mom and Dad are trying to hold her down and get her mouth open, and I'm bleeding all over the chair. I honestly thought she was going to take my thumb off, I swear."

"Christ."

"I'm telling you, for almost a week, this hand was the size of a boxing glove. Thirty-five stitches. No one really knows what people are capable of. That's one of the things that fascinates me about this field. People find themselves in situations that they would never have believed possible. It makes you question just how much control we have over ourselves."

Distractedly, I nod. A breeze comes through the parking lot, stirring up the trash in the gutters running along the edges, and Walter and I, as though acting on a cue, fall silent. I look back over my shoulder toward Julie's room. I can see her through the window, curled up into a ball on the bed like a frightened child.

"Julie bit me once," I say.

Walter looks at me, surprised. "Really."

"Yeah, back when she was six." I tell him about the time she'd wandered away from me in the Kmart kids' section while we were looking for back-to-school clothes. She'd walked around to the other side of the large circular clothing rack; the section was composed primarily of racks like this, and it made the area something of a labyrinth. Apparently, she'd believed that I was behind her because when she turned around and saw that I wasn't, she panicked and began dashing around, calling out for me. I chased after her, begging her to slow down and turn around, but in her frantic state she didn't realize that my voice was coming from directly behind her, and so I was never able to catch up. By the time I managed to grab her, she was sobbing hysterically; when I tried to pull her to me and hug her, she twisted away and swatted my face, not too hard, just enough to sting a little, to make her point. Then, when I'd finally managed to get my arms around her and I pulled her against me to calm her down, she bit me in the tender region between my shoulder and neck. Instinctively, I jerked away from her; this only made her cry louder.

"I wasn't even three feet from her the whole time I was chasing her," I say to Walter. "If she had just stopped and turned around, she would've seen me. But I couldn't get a hold of her. I chased her over half the damn store."

3.

It was sixth months ago that Ellen came across Walter's name in an online database of cult interventionists. "This is the guy, Lee!" she shrieked over the phone one afternoon after reading *Free At Last*, which she'd ordered off his website. "He's perfect! He's studied them, the Brethren I mean. And the way he writes, oh my god, it's like he knows her. Listen to this: 'Cult leaders seek out seemingly normal people who, for one reason or another, may be experiencing confusion over their identities. Their targets, though varied, tend to be young, well-educated men and women with rebellious tendencies that perhaps have yet to be realized. Group leaders are able to detect these tendencies and then effectively exploit them.'"

She was speaking, of course, of Julie, who, at that point, had been with the Brethren for just over six months. Ellen and I had been researching cult intervention strategies for about a month, ever since Julie had sent us each a handwritten letter explaining how, in light of the preparations that lay ahead for her, she had decided that it would be in her best interest to break off contact with us. Had it been up to Ellen, she probably would have hired the first person she came across. But as I pointed out to her, this wasn't something we could rush into; the wrong person could result in a fouled-up intervention, which might only drive Julie away further.

A couple weeks later, Ellen and I met for lunch at a small sandwich shop near her office to discuss our course of action. I'd purchased a used copy of the book online and had skimmed most of it, and I agreed with her that this man—Walter—would be perfect for us (assuming we could afford him; we didn't yet know what the going rate for a cult interventionist was, but we knew that it wouldn't be cheap), but I wasn't ready to take any action until we'd discussed it thoroughly.

"I emailed him already," she said, gulping down a mouthful of tuna-and-rye.

"I though we were going to talk first."

"It was just an email. I wanted to know his rates."

I mulled over a bite of my roast beef, pretending not to be bothered by her having taken the initiative. "Okay, so what did he say?"

She took a deep breath and made a face. "Nine thousand, plus travel expenses."

"Are you fucking serious?" I hissed, leaning across the table.

Ellen nodded glumly and wiped her fingers with a napkin. "I know. But you knew this was going to cost us. We both knew that. These specialists, I mean, would you expect anything less?"

Listening to the confident, almost condescending way she spoke about it, one might have gotten the impression she'd already been through a few dozen interventions. This has always been part of our dynamic: she speaks to me like a kid who needs things spelled out for him, and I do my best to hide the fact that this assumption is not entirely unjustified.

We spoke to Walter on the phone several times before arranging for him to fly in from Chicago for a formal meeting. Presently, he was spending a year as a Distinguished Fellow at DePaul. Ellen and I had to put him up in a hotel, though it was only for one night (I had suggested having him stay in the spare bedroom at her place, but Ellen said that would have been "unprofessional"). He pulled up to the house in a sleek silver rental. As he crossed Ellen's tidy little yard, carrying a leather satchel at his side, I was surprised by what I saw: a tall, athletic man with broad shoulders and shoulder-length brown hair, which had already begun to go grey, even though he couldn't have been more than forty. His face was long and angular, and he wore slim specs that sat smartly on his long nose. I'd seen pictures of him on his website, but in person he appeared much younger and much more self-possessed, like he'd just strolled out of a magazine ad for teeth whitener.

He introduced himself to us and gave mine and Ellen's hands each a firm pump and then daintily brushed his hair back behind his ears. "I'm sorry for running so late," he said. "I got all turned around out on Route 11."

"Happens to everyone," Ellen said reassuringly. "It's a tricky area if you aren't familiar with it. Please, come on inside. You want some coffee or tea or anything?"

Inside the house, the three of us sat in Ellen's living room chatting about Walter's background: born in Missouri, educated at Duke and Columbia. His doctoral dissertation, a two hundred-eighteen-page critique of the psychoanalytical techniques used on former members of the Branch Davidians, had become the foundation of his first book, *Lessons from Waco: What the Branch Davidians Can Teach us About Psychoanalysis*. There was a forced congeniality to the conversation, much like a job interview. And I guess that for Walter, this was actually sort of the case, which was weird for me; I wasn't used to being on this side of the interview.

After some time, Walter leaned forward in his seat and steepled the tips of his fingers beneath his nose, and I could see he was ready to get down to business. "Let me tell you a little about what I do," he said in a serious voice. "My job, as I see it, is not to deprogram people. I've always hated that term, it makes my clients sound like—I don't know—pieces of software." Here he paused briefly and flashed Ellen and me a small toothy smile, waiting, it seemed, for us to offer up a laugh or two at his joke, which we did, politely. "What I do is I give them the tools to deprogram themselves. I facilitate the transition back into the rational world."

Ellen and I exchanged a glance. *Facilitate. Rational. Transition.* His words had an elegant gleam to them, like they were cast in bronze, and for a moment, as I looked at him, I considered that a handful of people like him in my business would put me out of a job.

We discussed the various stages of thought reform therapy—if handled properly, he said, Julie's departure from the Brethren and her reentry into a normal life would be very similar to the stages of grief that usually accompany the death of a loved one—and his qualifications, even though Ellen and I were already familiar enough with them from his website: fifteen years in the field, a seventy-seven percent success rate, five books. "How are we supposed to go about getting her," he asked, "your daughter, I mean? Julie."

Ellen and I looked at one another apprehensively. "Well, that's sort of the big issue at the moment," she said. "We're not entirely sure we can get to her. We don't know of any way to get her off the compound."

"Right," he replied thoughtfully, again tucking his hair behind his ear. "Well, I've done a little bit of research on the property itself, and I know that the compound is accessible. I mean, there's no gate between the service road and the main road."

"So, wait. What are you suggesting?"

"I'm suggesting that we go get her."

"Is that legal?" I said.

He sat back and threw an arm over the back of the chair. "When there's reason to believe that the client's bodily health is in danger, then the law allows for involuntary removal from the premises. That's why we have social workers."

"But that's the thing," said Ellen, "We can't really prove that she's in any danger. It's not like Jonestown. There's no threat of mass suicide or anything like that."

"And we aren't social workers," I added.

"We could use the sleep deprivation pods as our just cause. Dehydration, malnutrition, forced isolation. We could make a case with that."

Ellen made a face. "Is that just cause enough?"

"It's really all we have," Walter said, crossing his legs. "And anyway, I doubt we'd really come up against any opposition. We go in, we get her. The group certainly won't press charges, and neither will she, not after I get into her head, bring her back to reality."

It made me uneasy, how offhandedly he talked about Julie and the intervention. Like an obstacle, something to be overcome. I glanced over at Ellen, looking down at her lap. To no one in particular I said: "I don't know how comfortable I am with that."

"There's nothing to be comfortable about," he replied. "It's an awful situation. But it's one that we're trying to remedy. And I'm telling you that, from my experience, you're not going to get her off that compound. Not willingly, anyway."

4.

That night Walter tells Ellen and me to go find someplace to grab a bite to eat so that we can clear our heads. "I'll keep an eye on her," he says, meaning Julie. "You two need to decompress." He taps his temple. "If it gets too cloudy in there, then you've got problems. Go unwind for a bit."

We find a seafood restaurant a mile down the road near the interstate onramp. (The diner would have been a much more practical choice, but the weird truth is that I liked having the place to myself, and the thought of letting Ellen in on it made me feel like I was giving up something I had earned). As the waitress—a plump redhead who looks to be around Julie's age—takes our drink orders, it occurs to me that this is the first time since the divorce that Ellen and I have shared a meal (not counting, of course, the birthday and graduation dinners with Julie). Now, sitting there across from her and watching her fumble with her napkin, I am reminded of those awkward, exhilarating dinners she and I had years back in college when we were first dating. I know folks who think back to those years and are stunned by how far away they seem. Centuries. Millennia. But for me, that period of time has always felt fresh and just kind of right there, and I don't know what that says about me, but I'd like to believe that it's an okay thing that I haven't readily abandoned our history, that it's something I still wear proudly, like an expensive but outdated suit.

"I don't like leaving her alone with him," Ellen says now. She is scanning the menu, though it's only for show: she'll eventually settle for a salad and a glass of iced tea. "He makes me nervous."

"It's what we're paying him for, to handle Julie."

"I know. It's just, I mean, it's like she's a prisoner or something, you know? I don't like it."

"What's to like about it?"

She sneers at me. "Don't do that."

"Do what?"

"That devil's advocate shit. You know what I'm trying to say."

The waitress returns with our drinks and sullenly takes our orders and then shuffles back into the kitchen. I watch her out of the corner of my eye; by the end of her shift, she will have already forgotten about us. Ellen gazes out the window, holding her chin in her palm like a crestfallen teenager, and I want someone to take a picture of this moment and hold it up next to a shot of us twenty-five years ago, a before-and-after kind of thing, so I can make some guess as to what the hell went wrong.

"If this thing works out," I say to her, "what happens afterward?"

"What do you mean?"

"I mean, what do we do? Does she move home, or does she go back to school, or what?"

"No idea," Ellen replies, her voice infused with a groan. She pinches the bridge of her nose. "I just want to be done with this. That's all I care about. I want my baby back."

I nod. Like my ex-wife, I want to believe that maybe there's some sort of formula we can fall back on, a way of isolating certain variables in Julie's history and then solving for x. This is really what hindsight is all about. But peoples' lives can't be quantified that way. There is too much randomness and not enough constants. As soon as you think you've figured it out, suddenly there's this brand new variable that throws everything out of whack and you've got to start all over again.

**

I was working part-time as a valet at the Montgomery County Country Club during my junior year of college when I met Ellen. She worked in the coat room, located in the large foyer of the immaculate white main building. When she wasn't tagging coats and handbags—most of which were worth more than what either of us would have made in months—she spent most of her time studying by the grim light of the old lamp on the desk at the back of the room. She wore long skirts and thin, gauzy blouses that were usually just tight enough to emphasize her exceptional breasts without seeming tacky. With her strawberry blonde hair pinned up into a clever bun, drawing attention to the creamy column of her neck, and with her black-framed reading glasses on, she looked like the Hollywood embodiment of the sexy librarian: smart and sophisticated, but not at the expense of her sexual energy.

On my breaks, I would sneak out of the valets' office up into the coat room to chat with her. Standing next to her desk, I would look down over her shoulder at whichever textbook she was poring over and pretend to offer advice. "You've got to carry the three," I'd joke, gazing at a page crammed full of complex equations and symbols. "It's a pretty simple mistake."

She'd throw me an annoyed smirk and then make a little shooing motion and say, "Shut up. Do you even go to class?"

"When the mood strikes me."

"And how often would that be?"

"I don't know, couple times a week maybe."

"Such a scholar."

It was like this for maybe six months, us ambling around each other. We got to know one another fairly well during this time. She told me about her mother, who had left her father for a paralegal named Claire when Ellen was thirteen. I told her about my older brother Kyle who had tried to kill himself in a Wal-Mart parking lot one night by running a piece of garden hose from the exhaust pipe of his truck into the front window, until a police officer passing by had spotted his taillights. Whether or not you'd call what Ellen and I had a relationship, I can't say, but it was something, and I relished it, partly because I found her intimidating, a constant challenge. I could never quite figure her out, which only made the desire to do so even stronger.

And maybe this was what kept me from asking her out for so long, the fear that her saying no would put an end to this thing that we'd cultivated. Also, talking to girls was a relatively new thing for me. I was only a few years out of high school; up until then I'd been a skinny kid with a bad complexion and a general fear of women. With the exception of a couple of girls I'd known through the school band, I had more or less avoided the issue all together. So, when I finally worked up the nerve to sputter it out—"So, you want to get coffee or something sometime? Or, like, dinner?"—she simply closed her book and sat back in her chair and gave me an appraising look, the way you might look at a toddler who's just done something adorable, and she said, "Finally. See? That wasn't so hard, now was it?"

By the time Julie came around, Ellen and I had been married for almost three years and were living in a small leaky rental house in Southwestern Virginia, where we'd come after Ellen had secured a position at an engineering firm that specialized in demolition. I had recently taken a job as a pharmaceutical rep for a small company that, within another five years, would ultimately go bankrupt. It was a job that sometimes kept me on the road for weeks at a time for very little pay, although Ellen and I were too young to realize that I was getting hosed. I had hoped that Julie's birth might dispel some of my growing insecurities about my marriage, the kinds of insecurities that all young married couples battle in secret, and for a while it actually did. There were vacations to plan and ear infections to be treated, school plays to attend and birthday parties to put together. We were happy, me and Ellen, or at least we believed that we were, which was enough for the time being.

Still though, there was always this lingering doubt that I was living a life I wasn't ready for, or hadn't earned. I could never get over the long flat fear that I was being strung along somehow, that eventually everything good in my life would vanish, dissipate. I knew that this had partly to do with my role as a father. I've heard men talk about the terror that comes with being a father, how you can look into your child's eyes and it's like someone taking your brain and shaking it like a snow globe, because suddenly every awful thing you've ever done comes racing back at you, every cruel word, every sabotaged relationship, every lie. You're confronted with the impossible scope of your responsibilities, and you understand that, invariably, you will fail your child in some way.

Of course, for all I know, Ellen was having these same feelings, or others very much like them, but the subject never came up. How could it? How can you tell your wife that just looking at your daughter makes you feel—what? Like a bad person? A failure? Regardless, I'm sure that it was this gnawing insecurity, at least on my part, that fueled most of our fights, which, after a number of years, became almost routine. A scratched fender would send us into an earsplitting shouting frenzy; an unkind inflection during a conversation would lead to several days' worth of the silent treatment. It all just became standard. And still I held out hope that we could fix it, that it was salvageable, our relationship. We were still young, weren't we? What did we know? We just had to keep working at it, was all.

Then there was the incident with Kathleen Barry, and that pretty much ruined everything.

Kathleen worked in the Atlanta branch of my company. Our sales circuits overlapped so that we would often find ourselves staying at the same hotels, and at the company's lackluster hotel conferences we were sometimes seated at the same table, where we would drink a little too much and maybe flirt some, though it was never anything more than a lingering hand on the shoulder or a few innuendos. She was like most of the other single women on my sales route: dowdy and disheveled, no matter how well she tried to manage herself, though the suave way she carried herself and the girlish glint in her eyes suggested that a very lovely woman had once lived in her small body. She wore business skirts and blouses that drew attention to her chest and hips while also making her look worn-out and a bit lonely. She was divorced, a fact she was always prone to remind me of after a few glasses of wine.

That we only saw each other a few times a year added to the excitement I felt whenever one of those opportunities arose. I told myself on these occasions that we were just friends, me and Kathleen, a couple of road-weary salespeople lumped together in an unfamiliar place, and that as such, our flirting was not only good-natured but also necessary in order to make the travel bearable.

Actually, the flirting, such as it was, was mostly on Kathleen's part. This was all part of our arrangement. She knew how much I looked forward to seeing her—I didn't have to tell her—and she reveled in her ability to stir such a reaction in me, whether it was by placing a hand on my bicep when she laughed at one of my jokes as if to steady herself or by casually referencing the color of her underwear, making me blush. "You'd be a lot more attractive if you were single," she told me once at some convention in Raleigh, throwing back her fourth glass of pinot noir, to which I smiled and giggled and played bashful. This was how I always reacted to Kathleen's advances: it was the only way to keep her at bay while ensuring that the attention wouldn't stop. I never bothered reminding her that I was a married man; I was pretty sure that was the point.

One night we'd been drinking in the downstairs bar of the Knoxville Doubletree, a dark, smoky little room lit almost exclusively by these tiny paper sconces on the tables. In the corner, a jazz trio plinked out a sublime version of "God Bless the Child." At some point, I told Kathleen that I was going to head up to my room to go to bed. I could feel that tension building between us again, heavy and warm, and so I was trying to be responsible by removing myself from the situation. "Yeah, I think I'll do the same," she said, smoothing her grey skirt over her fleshy stocking thighs. We were staying on the same floor, just a few doors down from one another.

Of course I knew what she was doing—she wasn't tired in the least, and would probably have been content to stay down in the bar for another hour, tossing back drinks and listening to the band. But the fact is that people like Kathleen—who have been so wrecked by their own relationships that they're determined to see everyone else's wrecked, too—and people like me—who are too foolish to keep their own relationships from being wrecked—can't keep up the act for too long before something bad happens. And had I been a decent human being who was even remotely worthy of the love of his wife and daughter, I would have sat her down then and said, No, Kathleen, I know how this ends, and while I think you're a terrific woman, I am married, and so for the sake of our friendship and for my marriage, please do not get in that elevator with me.

But I didn't say this.

I wanted her to follow me up there, and she knew I wanted this. We were in that bad territory, where the absence of language becomes a language all its own. I told myself that I didn't know what she was planning, but I did—of course I did!—and as soon as we had made it up to the fifth floor, all my fears were confirmed when Kathleen, smelling strongly of wine and perfume and cigarette smoke, took a piece of my shirt between her knuckles and then pulled herself toward me, gathering up a fistful of fabric in the process, and kissed me. I wanted to pull back, push her away from me and run, or at least this was my instinct, but instead I returned the kiss, wrapping my arms around her and bringing her soft squarish body against mine. Then, when she knew she had me, she took a step back and smiled and ushered me into her room.

I'd like to be able to say that this was all Kathleen—that I'd been taken advantage of in some sinister way, but the fact is I knew precisely what I was doing: I had come to believe that I didn't deserve the life I'd constructed for myself and so now, in an act of misdirected self-destruction, I was trying to knock it all down.

It wasn't until I'd made it back home several days later that I would come to find that Ellen had tried to call me in my room that night. Julie had started puking, some kind of viral infection, according to the pediatrician. Of course, having spent most of the night in Kathleen's room, I didn't get any of the calls. Ellen asked me where I had been, and it wasn't unkind or suspicious, just earnest in a way that made the knots in me come loose all at once, and suddenly I found myself confessing everything to her, and not just what had happened with Kathleen that night, but my entire history with her, such as it was. I couldn't help myself, couldn't stop, not even when Ellen began shrieking at me between sobs to get the hell out of the house.

It wasn't long after this that I moved out into a small apartment across town—a temporary thing, I told myself, just until Ellen and I got this awful business sorted out. But it didn't take long for me to realize that there was nothing to sort out, that I had simply confirmed whatever suspicions Ellen had had about my investment in the marriage. It took a year for us to finalize the divorce. That Ellen and I have remained friends, or friendly at least, over the past twelve years isn't so much proof of her forgiving nature—though that's certainly part of it—but more an indication of how she's truly come to regard me: I am something that happened to her, a problem resolved. I'm not worth the effort of a grudge.

5.

By the next morning, Julie's already crawled out from behind the bed. She eats her breakfast—another round of goopy eggs and toast and fruit from the diner—seated on the bed with her legs crossed. Of course none of us mentions this—we don't want to scare her off with any sudden moves—though Ellen and Walter and I are all three watching her closely out of the corners of our eyes. I can see from the long deep shadows in her neck and the crisp line of her jaw just how much weight she's lost, although she still insists on picking lightly at her food. I'd almost rather see her cram it all into her mouth at once, contest-style.

When she's finished eating, she wipes her fingers on the hem of her tunic and then, slowly and shakily, she stands and heads for the bathroom, grabbing the jeans and shirt that Ellen set out for her on the basin of the sink. "I'm going to take a shower," she says, peering at us backward in the large mirror, running her fingers through her oily hair. It's clear that much of the animosity we saw in her yesterday has dried up, or at least been put aside in favor of food and clean clothes. Ellen and I nod. As soon as the door closes and we hear the hiss of the water, I feel the strength leave my legs and I sink down onto the bed. Ellen, too.

"That's good, right?" she whispers. She looks from me, to Walter, and then back to me.

"Dissociation shock," Walter mutters dismissively, rummaging through his duffel bag. He retrieves a bottle of No-Doz and with one hand he pops the cap and then taps a few out of the bottle into his mouth. "She'll experience a mild depressive state, characterized by strong feelings of guilt and alienation." Swallowing two of the pills, he winces. I recognize this term, dissociation shock. Chapter five: "What to Expect from Your Exit Counselor."

Today is phase two, the Renunciation phase. Walter and Julie spend most of the morning sifting through Walter's tub of information, deconstructing various pieces of Cosmic Brethren literature, pamphlets and testimonials from other members and a few small news articles from the *Charlottesville Courier*, which has kept more or less steady tabs on the Brethren for the past few years, hungrily anticipating some Jonestown-scale mass suicide to generate a shitload of copy. Walter reads aloud the entire ten-page Cosmic Brethren manifesto, which he printed off the website. The document outlines the group's sorrow over the current state of human affairs and their eagerness to begin anew someplace far away. Every so often he pauses and asks how she feels about a particular section, what she takes it to mean, whether or not she believes it to be accurate. And each time, Julie will wrinkle her brow and rub her chin or nibble her fingernails, seeming to contemplate the question, although it isn't long before I start to suspect that these reactions aren't entirely genuine, that she's just placating Walter, maybe just to move things along, get it all over with. Whether or not Walter notices any of this, I don't know, but I stay quiet. Walter doesn't like interruptions.

There's a one-hour lunch break at noon, during which we finish the pizza from yesterday. Already the room has taken on the gamey odor of grease and sleep-deprived bodies. The whole experience is beginning to feel a little like camping. After lunch Ellen slinks back to her room for a short nap; her eyes are pinched at the corners and underscored by purple splotches, and I can tell she's desperate for some rest. Meanwhile, Walter, still strikingly alert, takes a walk around the motel to stretch his legs. Of the four of us, he's the only one who doesn't look as though he's been awake for three days in a row. Julie lays on her belly on the bed, her head resting on her folded arms, while I sprawl out in one of the chairs, flipping idly through the TV stations, though I have no idea what I'm looking for. After some time, she sits up and tucks her hair behind her ears. "Do you guys hate me?" she says.

I look over at her, confused and a little hurt by the implication that I'm even capable of hating her. Although, at the same time, it's thrilling to hear her talk like this again, like a normal girl, like Julie and not some would-be space cadet. "Of course not. Why would you ask that?"

"Just the school thing, dropping out and all that." She shrugs. "And the car, too. You were pretty upset about it."

"Upset, sure, but I don't hate you."

With a heavy sigh, she looks up at the ceiling. "They're not bad people, Dad."

"I didn't say they were."

"But that's what you think. You think they're lunatics or something."

I nod. "I won't argue with that."

She gives me a cool and honest gaze, and there goes my heart, revving like a little motor. She's got her mother's eyes, a rich glassy green color, and when she smiles they crinkle up at the edges like pieces of candy. "You don't think there's a chance, I mean, just a tiny possibility that they might be right? Is it really that far-fetched?"

There's a feeling like something's slipping here, like something's getting away from me, and I almost detect that robotic defiance creeping back into her voice. "Honey, I don't know. I don't think I want to know."

She lies back down on her stomach. "Maybe that's your problem."

**

I'm watching a movie in my room later that night, some urban combat thing with Bruce Willis, when there's a knock at the door. Instinctively, I bolt upright on the bed, believing for an instant that the rest of the Brethren have tracked us down and have come to reclaim Julie. And so naturally I'm relieved, after slipping my jeans on and opening the door with a forced and probably creepy look of openness on my face, to see Ellen standing there, barefoot, gazing down at the walkway with her arms crossed. At first I'm not really sure what to say. When was the last time she came looking for me? It's slightly thrilling and slightly unnerving at the same time.

"Couldn't sleep," she says softly, tucking a wisp of hair behind her ear, and then, after a pause, "These beds are terrible."

I laugh through my nose and nod. "My sheets smell like cigarettes."

"Lovely."

There's a couple more seconds of us just standing there—her waiting for me to invite her in, me trying to figure out whether or not I'm supposed to invite her in—before she brushes past me into the room, where, without a word, she sinks down onto the end of the bed, clasping her hands between her knees. Suddenly, it's like we're back to our old signals, because I close the door and walk over and sit down beside her, close enough so that she can lay her head on my shoulder, which she does, as if this was planned all along. Like we just know. We don't talk; we don't have to. When you're with someone for a certain period of time, you grow fairly adept at deciphering the various modes of silence that arise during moments of extreme gravity, the unspoken overtures and concessions like the buzzing of nerves before a storm, and it's by this measure, presumably, that Ellen, her face drawn into a look of weary contemplation, now stands and slips delicately out of her jeans and sweater and underwear and then, with what seems to be a conscious lack of intimacy, shrugs and holds up her palms: *Who cares?* In a small, distant voice she says: "I just need to be here now for a little bit, if that's okay."

"What about Julie?"

"She's asleep. She'll be okay, you think?"

I scratch the back of my neck. "Yeah, probably."

And so this is how I find myself lying naked with my ex-wife on a foul-smelling motel bed, looking over her body with a kind of childlike fascination. It's like visiting the city you grew up in after years of being away, the sobering juxtaposition of familiar places with new ones. I notice the plumpness of her belly and hips, the tiny hairs around her nipples, the scarlike veins in her thighs—things that, in theory, I'm supposed to think of as unattractive, but I don't. If anything, the evidence of age in her body only makes her seem more beautiful, elegant in a way that could only have developed over time. Not like me, with my pale rubbery midsection and the patches of hair all over my back and shoulders. As I lay there tracing the gentle slope of Ellen's collar bone with my fingertip, I think about the Zetas zipping about the galaxy in their super-advanced ships, observing the spectacle of human interaction, and I can't help but wonder what they might make of me and Ellen at this moment, whether the sight of these two broken human beings laying side-by-side on a bed in some dirty motel room has any bearing on their opinion of the human race.

But—what is it? Something doesn't feel right. As I lay there beside Ellen, feeling the cool sturdy weight of her expectation, I keep going back to what Julie said earlier today. *Maybe that's your problem.* The whole thing's got me so tied up in the head that I'm finding it hard to concentrate on the situation at hand, my lovely ex-wife in bed next to me, waiting, waiting. Plus, there's the whole big pain-in-the-ass issue of how we're going to feel about this in the morning: obviously, there's some potential here for us to completely fuck up the intervention, all the progress we've made with Julie so far, and I know for Ellen this is maybe one of those any-port-in-a-storm kind of things, that it doesn't have a lot to do with me. But then what happens tomorrow when we go back into Julie's room and try to persuade her that she's deluding herself, chasing a fantasy that will never pay off the way she wants? I'd like to believe that our present situation is somehow more sophisticated—but how?

Finally, Ellen props herself up onto her elbows and looks over at me. I can't tell if the expression on her face is amusement or pity, though I suspect it's some combination of both. "You're not going to do anything, are you?" The way she says it is more of a statement than a question.

I run my fingers up her leg and over her left breast, feeling the muted pulse of her breath.

"No."

She falls back on her pillow. "Well then."

A few feet away, the television crackles with the sounds of gunfire and screaming, but it feels like it's coming from someplace far away. I should be angry with myself, or disappointed, something. But I'm not.

I nuzzle my head against her and she puts her arm around me like a mother comforting a child, and I lay there breathing in the tangy combination of smells of Ellen's skin. Citrus. Salt. Powder. By the time the movie ends I'm already in that tenuous place between awake and sleep where the body disappears completely and the mind is left to charge blindly through the dark, and so I don't make any moves when Ellen carefully climbs off the bed and puts her clothes back on and slips out of the room without a word, and before I roll over onto my back and fall asleep completely, I consider for just a moment the possibility that I imagined her ever being here at all.

6.

I awake to the sound of rain, fat heavy sheets of it hammering the parking lot outside. The digital clock beside the bed says 5:49AM. Why I'm up so early, I have no idea, but I'm actually kind of thankful for the opportunity to have a few hours to myself before the intervention starts back up. I need to think about what happened with Ellen last night.

I run the toothbrush over my mossy teeth for a few seconds and then put my jeans and shirt back on and step out onto the damp covered walkway. A thick stream of dirty brown water flows through the center of the parking lot toward the drainage ditch running between the motel and the diner. The gray-green mountains in the distance are mottled by wispy fog clouds the same color as the sky so that from where I'm standing it appears as though someone took a giant eraser to them but then gave up halfway through. Walter and Ellen and Julie probably won't be up for another hour or so, and so in the meantime I trot across the parking lot in the rain toward the diner, trying my best to avoid the divots in the weathered blacktop where water has pooled, though my shoes are still soaked by the time I make it to the door.

Inside, it's just the same ancient waitress and a couple of cooks, all of them seated at the counter, puffing away on cigarettes and gazing sleepily down into their coffee mugs. When they see me enter, the cooks pry themselves out of their seats and, coffee cups in hand, plod around the side of the counter toward the kitchen, back to work. Naturally, I feel a little guilty, like I'm gobbling up their break time. But not enough to run back through the rain to my room.

"How you doing, Hon?" the waitress calls out as she ties the strings of her dingy white apron around her.

"I'm here. I guess," I reply, straddling one of the stools at the counter.

A moment later she shuffles over with a cup of coffee and a tiny dish of half-and-half packets. "You on vacation or something?" she says. Behind her, I can see the two cooks watching me from over the ledge, no doubt praying for me to order something quick and simple so that they can go back to their morning coffees.

I'm about to shake my head, say *No, not quite*, when almost instantly I realize that I don't have a plausible cover story; why would anyone spend three nights at the I-64 Budget Lodge?

"Business," I mumble, offering her a coy grin-and-eye-roll combination, hoping maybe she won't bother with the questions if I act like it's boring business, and at the same time I'm kicking myself for not having come up with some sort of lie I could sputter out if anyone asks about what we're doing here, a cover story. Not that I anticipated needing to use it; it's just good planning.

"What business you in?"

"Sales. I'm in sales."

She nods, slowly and thoughtfully, seeming to understand that I'm being intentionally vague. Her flat bluish eyes, cloudy and glazed, suggest a history of dealing with customers with unfortunate histories, people with things to hide, and so she understands it's best not to pursue the issue.

I ask what her name is. "Phyllis," she says.

"I'm Lee."

"Good to meet you, Lee."

"Yeah, you too. How long you been working here?"

She taps a chewed-up pencil against the counter. "A few years. About five, I think."

"You like it?"

"I suppose," she says, cocking her head, making the fleshy white folds of her neck bulge. "It's a job. It's a paycheck. Why you ask?"

"I was just curious. I didn't mean anything by it."

She looks me over warily, and I can tell that she feels a little sorry for me. It's a look I've gotten accustomed to after so many years of traveling, a kind of pitying appraisal, the sort of look one might give to a teenage runaway. "You like your job?" she says finally.

I shrug and pour creamer in my coffee. "Sometimes. I like meeting new people. And I get to travel a lot, which is nice. But I guess it gets a little old, always moving around so much. You start feeling cut off from the world."

She props a chubby fist on her hip. "My oldest boy, he drives a rig, and he says that's the toughest part of the job, the getting lonely." Her voice is softer now, almost motherly. "He says some people are just supposed to be that way though, you know? They just work better alone, he says."

"That makes sense." I pick up one of the half-and-halfs, drop it back into the dish. "I don't know if I'm one of those people, though."

"Maybe you're in the wrong business then."

I laugh. "Maybe."

She asks me what I would like to eat, and I order a plate of scrambled eggs and toast and a side of grits, and as the woman drops the pencil into her apron pocket, I glance over at the two cooks—still leering at me—trying to gauge their reactions to my order.

Later, as the others are eating their breakfasts back in the room, I'm watching Julie, who is seated Indian-style at the head of the bed, dressed in a pair of khaki shorts and a blue t-shirt, with her container of food in her lap, and I'm marveling over all the progress she's made in the past couple days. This doesn't seem like the zombielike girl we snatched out of the peach orchard nights earlier; this girl's cheeks have a lively pinkish tint to them, and she's more prone to smile—all of this as Ellen gives her a rundown of which of her friends from high school have gotten married or had kids or both. We leave the room door open while we eat so we can watch the rainfall, the eighteen-wheelers eeking past on the slick highway beyond the parking lot.

When we've finished eating, I ask Ellen if she'll help me carry the trash out to the dumpsters. "Just put it in the trash can," she says.

"I want to go ahead and get it out of here. It's going to start to smell."

She makes a face and then rolls her eyes and gives a drawn-out "Okaaaaay," and she and I gather up that morning's trash and head for the door. Walter raises an eyebrow at me as I hold the door for Ellen, and then he begins sifting through his bag for his No-Doz.

"I wanted to ask about last night," I say as the two of us carry the trash across the parking lot.

"Last night?"

"Yeah. You know, what happened."

"Right."

"I just want to make sure that we're okay today, you and me. I mean, I want to know that things are, you know, okay. And I wanted to explain my, you know, reluctance."

She stops and turns to me, laughing. "Is that why you wanted me to come out here?"

"Sort of."

"Look, Lee, we're big kids. I needed someone to be there, and that happened to be you. It's not that complicated."

"Okay, but just—"

"Just stop worrying about it," she cuts in, smiling. "It doesn't change anything, if that's what you're thinking. You don't have to *do* anything." She accentuates this with a playful fluttering of her fingers. "I understand, really. You were being cautious. It's probably better anyway that nothing happened. Less for us to have to think about."

"Probably." Though this doesn't really make me feel any better.

When we get back to the room, Walter begins the session. "Okay, Julie," he says with his customary calmness, "I want you to know that we all understand how tough these past few days have been for you, and we want you to know how proud we are of you." He pauses here, presumably for effect, and it occurs to me that I won't be surprised if, in five years, I happen to come across him on *Oprah*. Ellen squeezes Julie's shoulder and nods encouragingly. I smile: the two women in my life. Walter goes on, "If you remember, I asked you the other day if you knew why you were here. Do you remember? I was hoping maybe you'd be willing to try to answer that question now."

Behind us, the ancient AC unit clatters to life. I'm watching Julie nibble her fingernails—an old habit, one I'm so happy to see that I'm tempted to jump in there and nibble them with her—thinking the question over like a contestant on a game show. That's sort of how this whole thing is starting to feel, like a game show, something with absurd stakes that, even if I wanted to watch something else, I wouldn't be able to. It's the lack of sleep, I guess, and the substandard food; I'm fighting through the fog in my head, trying to stay focused.

Julie takes a breath to speak, and when she does, her words are stretched out and punctuated with pensive silences like she's choosing them very carefully. "I suppose I'm here because…you all are…concerned, I guess…that I've made…a very…unhealthy… decision here to join the Brethren, because…you think…it's a scam?"

I wasn't around for Julie's first word—I was in Midland, Texas, I remember, hocking a titanium kneecap to a conference room of underwhelmed orthopedic surgeons—but I imagine that, had I been there, the feeling would have been a lot like the one that washes over me now in the two-to-three seconds of stunned quiet that fill the room now, before finally Walter sits back and nods slowly and says, "That's fantastic, Julie. Really good. You've done so well."

7.

Tonight I've offered to stay in Julie's room. I figure it's only fair considering that Ellen spent the past two nights with her. "You sure you're up for it?" Ellen asked in a sardonic voice when I told her.

"That's kind of a shitty thing to say," I replied.

"Sorry. You know I didn't mean it like that."

"Maybe you should leave me a list of contact numbers, just in case."

"Come on, don't be a baby. I was just asking."

Julie lies on her stomach on the bed and I sit beside her; we're watching some ridiculous reality program, a bunch of former celebrities have to start a business together, something. Tomorrow is the final day of the intervention, the Acceptance phase. I know we're both thinking about this, wondering what will happen once the whole ordeal is finished, but neither of us says anything, and I'm not sure if this is a conscious decision or not. We've always had difficulty communicating, Julie and me—though show me a father and a daughter who haven't. It's always a chase, trying to figure out your kids, who they really are. You can never truly know them, not in the way that you'd like. This is why they grow up and leave, because on some level you'll always be strangers to one another.

During a commercial, I look over at Julie, who's staring at the TV with a vacant look in her eyes like she's sitting through a biology lecture. I can't tell if she's tired or just bored by the program or what, though it doesn't appear to have occurred to her to change the channel. When she notices me watching at her she cocks her head and grins suspiciously and says, "What?"

"What was it?" I say.

"What was what?"

"The, I don't know, the thing that made you leave. What, I guess, compelled you to join up with them?" It's a question that up until now I haven't been able to ask her, either because I hadn't yet ascertained the scope of her involvement with the group or because she had already stopped communicating with me and Ellen, and it's maddening in its simplicity. I feel like it's something I shouldn't even have to ask.

She smiles now, and it's more wise and knowing than I've ever seen on anybody, the way the bottoms of her eyes flatten out and her lips sort of pucker. She looks like she's trying not to laugh. "It's hard to explain," she says quietly, tucking a wisp of hair behind her ear.

"What was so bad about your life that you wanted to leave it behind?"

"Dad, stop. You're oversimplifying. It's not that easy."

"I'm trying to understand."

"I know, but what I'm telling you is that I don't know if it can be explained that easily, you know? I mean, yes, obviously I gave it a lot of thought, and I knew what they were, the group. I really did. And I knew how you guys would react. But then I started looking at it in practical terms, like, what would I be losing, what would I be gaining, and at the time I did believe in their mission. Maybe I still do. I probably always will, a little bit, just because I think it's genuinely good."

"But what's good about it?" I say. "This is what I'm trying to get my head around. I don't see how 'good' can apply to what they do."

She looks up at the ceiling and grunts, frustrated. I probably should have kept my mouth shut, but we're off now, and I feel like I owe it to her to try and make sense of all this. "You guys can't see it in the context that I do. Or did, I guess." Her tone is crisp and direct, professorial. "You only see it as a bunch of aliens coming to whisk people off to a new planet. Like something out of a bad movie, that's your interpretation. But, I mean, I can't explain the appeal. There aren't really words for it, you know? That's sort of the point. The idea that these completely benevolent beings, that they might come and take us to a new beautiful place to let us start over and create the world the way it should be, it's such a beautiful thought, I can't even…I don't know…" Drawing her knees up to her chest, she rests her forehead on them and shuts her eyes, and I see a tear slide down the side of her face.

I sit up on my knees and wrap my arms around her and bury my face in her hair. "I'm sorry. I didn't mean to upset you." I kiss the top of her head and nuzzle my cheek against it. When she was a baby, I used to go into her room at night sometimes and lift her out of her crib and smell her head: it had a sweet unassuming scent, like vanilla and soap.

She wipes her nose with the back of her hand and snivels wetly. Then she grabs onto my arm and leans her head against mine. "It's not easy for me, Dad, okay?" she stutters. "I don't know what's going happen."

"I know."

She lies down on her side facing the wall. I lie down next to her and rest my head on my shoulder. I feel terrible. There are no words for moments like these, or at least none worth using. My daughter, my baby girl. The body just isn't big enough for love.

After a while we drift off. I can still hear the warble of the television, but I'm only aware of it in a distant peripheral sense, the way that the mind incorporates real-world sounds into dreams. When I wake up the digital clock on the nightstand says 3:20. Julie's snoring in that soft nasally way that I know means she's sound asleep. Easing myself off the bed, I gently pull the covers up over her and then, when I'm satisfied that she won't be up for some time, I step outside for some air.

The rain has left the air thick and damp and chilly. The broken asphalt of the parking lot is glazed with a layer of moisture. There's a dense fog that makes everything appear out of focus, otherworldly. This, combined with the lateness of the hour, seems to call out to my more erratic impulses, like a kind of drug. I look in the window at Julie, sleeping soundly under the covers. Then I feel my pockets for my keys.

A quick drive, I tell myself, just to clear my head.

I take the highway out in the direction of the compound. The roads are slick and shrouded in a haze of ghostly steam. Driving is a big part of my job, but it's been a long time since I've done it aimlessly, and it's a good feeling. I'm reminded of when Julie was a baby, how I used to take her for late-night rides in her car seat at night when she got fussy and couldn't sleep. We'd cruise around the neighborhood and then through the town and back home, and it occurs to me now that those were some of the happiest nights of my life: the close darkness of the car, Julie cooing and whimpering in the car seat until she finally passed out. Whoever it was who first discovered that driving could calm a crying child must have been the happiest person in the history of the world.

I pull off the highway and take the gravel road through the trees, until I reach the service road surrounding the orchard, where I stop the car. In the sallow light of the headlamps, the rows of peach trees seem larger and more imposing then they did days earlier, an army of brutish creatures poised to march. Up ahead at the bottom of the slope, there are a few lights on in some of the windows of the compound, but I'm guessing that most of the Brethren are either asleep or getting in their hours in the sensory deprivation pods.

I turn off the car and climb out. The air is brisk and sweet, but with a touch of something bitter and mulchy. Standing in the middle of the narrow dirt road, looking down through the trees at the compound, I think about Julie curled up on the bed back at the motel, sleeping soundly. I want to believe that this intervention was the right thing for us to do, and for the most part I do. But there's some part of me that remains skeptical. Was she trying to sabotage her life, assert her own destructive capacity, the same way I did years ago with Ellen? And if that's the case, am I really in a position to tell her otherwise?

Behind me, the pine trees rustle in the breeze, shaking off the water from that morning's rains. I turn and shuffle back to the car. As I'm climbing in, I hear something moving in the brush nearby, and I freeze with one foot in the car, the other on the cold red dirt. I stare down in the direction of the sound, wondering who would be skulking around the woods at this hour and what they'll do if they find me. Moments later, a small whitish creature emerges from the dense brush lining the road—a possum, its tiny black eyes gleaming diffidently in the moonlight. I don't move for fear of frightening it off. Angling its stubby pink snout upward, the crea-ture sniffs the air and then, when it has determined that the coast is clear, scuttles across the dirt road into the peach trees, followed by three babies, their tiny round bodies bobbing frantically and their long wormlike tails flicking back and forth as they vanish into the shadows on the other side of the dirt road.

**

It's close to four in the morning by the time I make it back to the motel.

I've been thinking a lot about what Walter said the other day in the parking lot, about people finding themselves in situations they never thought possible. Ellen used to complain about how I couldn't adapt to change; she said it was like I had this extremely narrow and undetailed idea of the way things are supposed to be, and any change to that idea turned me into one of those nervous old ladies who spends all day peering fearfully out their front window. I always scoffed at this, but the other night when she showed up at my door? I completely froze. I can't be sure why. It's a problem: everything catches me off guard.

And so I shouldn't be so surprised, upon pulling back into the parking lot next to Walter's Acura and then tiptoeing into the room, to find that Julie, having been left alone for the better part of an hour, has fled.

But of course I am.

8.

"You left her?" Walter growls at me.

"She was asleep. I heard her snoring."

"Oh, you heard her snoring!" he replies, throwing his hands in the air. "Well, you can't get much more definite than that!"

"Lower your voice. Jesus."

We're standing in Julie's room, me and him and Ellen, moments after I've roused them out of theirs. We're trying to figure out what we should do, what we *can* do. I've just spent the past forty-five minutes tromping through the dark woods behind the motel in search of Julie, only to wind up with a roadmap of red cuts and scrapes on my arms from the dense thorny foliage. After that, I ran about a quarter of a mile up the road hoping, perhaps, to catch her hitchhiking, but of course she was nowhere to be found. After I'd resigned myself to this fact, I paced the parking lot for a few minutes, trying to come up with a story; Julie attacked me and ran off, or maybe she slipped out while I was in the bathroom. But you can't go making up lies about your kid like that, and anyway nothing I came up with seemed remotely plausible, especially given the progress she'd made over the past two days.

And really, that's what makes her disappearance such a shock, the fact that she was doing so well. Was she just stringing us along, planning her escape? Why did she have to do it on my watch? Was she counting on me to give her an out? I can't help feeling like I've been betrayed.

Now the first traces of early blue are seeping into the morning sky; in another half hour or so the sun will creep up over the mountains.

"I'm calling the police." Ellen says, reaching for the phone.

"Why would you do that?" says Walter.

"Why not?"

"What are you going to tell them? 'My daughter, who I snatched illegally from the Cosmic Brethren compound, has vanished'?"

Despondently, Ellen sets the phone back on the cradle. She presses her hands to either side of her head, stretching the skin back on her face. She says, "But they'd understand, wouldn't they? They'd help find her, at least, right?" She wants to believe this, but it's clear that she doesn't. She knows what kind of position we're in, she just isn't ready to believe it yet.

I start fumbling around the room, moving stuff around like I'm hunting for my keys or something, just trying to make myself feel useful. "Maybe she's already talked to the police, do you think?" I say.

"She's not going to the police," Walter says in a churlish, condescending way, as though I'd suggested that perhaps Julie had simply sprouted wings and flown away, and for whatever reason, I suddenly remember what I said to Ellen a year ago about the author photo on the dust jacket of his book: *He looks like everybody I ever hated in high school.* He turns around now and faces me, hands on his hips. "Why would she do that? Why would she run to the police? She doesn't want to deal with them anymore than we do. If she's going anywhere, it's back to the compound."

Ellen's face lights up. "Well, we could still find her then, couldn't we? She's probably not that far."

"That depends," says Walter, looking over at me. "What time did you go for your drive, Superdad?"

"What the hell does that mean?" I say. Ellen throws him an impatient look. "She was asleep. Sound fucking asleep. I was gone like half an hour."

"You were gone, is the point, Lee. You left. Doesn't matter how long. You left her alone, and now she's gone."

I look over at Ellen. "You left her the other night. She was fine, wasn't she? Why wouldn't she run off then?"

Walter's eyes go wide. "Wait a second," he says, turning to face Ellen, "when did you leave her?"

Crossing her arms, Ellen gazes down at the carpet. "It was last night. It wasn't a big deal. I just needed to get out of the room for a while."

"Where did you go?"

"What does it matter?"

"She was in my room," I say. "We were talking."

Ellen glares at me. I pretend not to notice.

"Oh, okay, good," Walter says. "No, this is really good. So, you've both been leaving her alone, despite my instructions not to do so under any circumstances, and now here we are at an intervention without a client, and you're surprised that she ran off? Terrific."

"You need to stop now," I say. "This isn't helping."

"Excuse me, Lee, but you're hardly in a position to lecture me about helping."

"You're under contract to us. We're still paying you."

"I'm only under contract so long as the contracting party adheres to the guidelines. A violation nullifies the contract. It's in there, read it."

I glance over at Ellen for support, but she's giving me a steely sideways look that suggests she thinks I'm hiding something. I'm beginning to feel like Frankenstein staring down a sea of angry villagers armed with torches and pitchforks.

"Hold up," I say, taking a nervous step backward and holding my hands up defensively. "Do you think I wanted to let her go? Is that what you're suggesting?"

"I'm saying that you willingly gave her an opportunity to escape, yes. I'm suggesting it."

"This is fucking ridiculous."

"What's ridiculous is that all you had to do was stay here and look after your daughter. But you two can't seem to control yourselves long enough—"

It doesn't register with me at first that I've shoved him, not until he staggers backward and trips against the corner of the bed and I watch him somersault head over heels onto the floor. Out of the corner of my eye, I see Ellen cover her mouth with her hands.

I've got about two seconds of guilty satisfaction before he's on his feet and charging me, hands outstretched as though he's wandering through the dark. His face is flushed, and his eyes, bright and glistening, are full of a sad sort of bravado. He looks both terrified and profoundly angry, and it dawns on me, within that tiny fleeting moment, that what I'm seeing here is the real Walter Shapiro: a frightened, unhappy little man, stripped of his aura of brute intellectualism. He's just as out of place as the rest of us. And the fact that Walter seems achingly aware of how exposed he is to us now only magnifies this realization, so that we feel connected in some terrible way by a kind of knowledge that neither of us really wants.

But before he has a chance to get his clumsy hands on me, Ellen appears in front of me and slaps his face hard enough to make him stumble backward again, though this time he manages to stop and steady himself against the bed before tumbling backward, and then he brings a shaky hand to his face. There's a thin sheen of tears in his eyes. My first instinct is to smile.

That's when she turns and slaps me, too.

"This is goddamn pointless!" she snarls as Walter and I cradle our throbbing jaws, too stunned to even move; we just gape at her like a couple of scolded kids. "We're wasting time here, so knock it the fuck off!"

Walter and I stare at each other for a moment and then look

away. The only sound in the room is the AC unit humming and clanking, indifferent to our crisis. Ellen stomps over to the window and flings open the ratty curtains and gazes out at the parking lot. The sun is up, a pink sphere hanging low in the sky above the mountains in the distance.

Turning to Walter, I mutter, "Sorry."

He puffs up his cheeks and then exhales. "It's fine. Me too."

Maybe we mean it and maybe we don't, but it's as sincere as we're going to get, at least for now. I almost feel bad for the guy, it's impossible not to. Here we are, having been holed up in a crummy motel for the past three days, our nerves like fried-out fuses, living off of junk food and caffeine. Who wouldn't come unraveled?

Walter's eyes, still alight with a kind of desperation, dart back and forth in his head, as if searching for a way out.

"We should go look for her," I say. "We've got two cars. Walter's and mine."

"We'll need someone to stay here, in case she comes back," Walter says gloomily.

"You said she wasn't coming back," says Ellen. "You said she was going back to the compound. That's what you said."

"She might come back. Look, it's better to have somebody here, is all I'm saying. Just in case."

Ellen and I decide that she should take the car while I stay back at the motel, her rationale being, I suppose, that it was my driving that got us here in the first place, and I'm not really in a position to argue.

Once we've settled on the plans, Walter moves for the door. "I'll head out toward the compound. If I see her, Lee, I'll call your cell, okay?"

"Okay."

He steeples his fingers beneath his nose, the same way he did during our first face-to-face meeting at Ellen's house, and he steps in close to me, his head bowed. "I apologize for my behavior. I'm tired and out of sorts. It was uncalled for." He's about as convincing as a bowtie on a dog.

I tell him it's okay and that the same goes for me, which is more or less true at this point; it's not really Walter I'm pissed at, anyway. Is he someone I'd want to go out for beers with? Not quite.

But if the day ever comes when I do see him on *Oprah*, I'll watch the entire segment.

With this, he nods, affecting a forced formalness, and he heads out to search for Julie.

When he's gone, Ellen goes to the sink and splashes water on her face.

"Jesus," I say, "can you believe that?"

She angles her mouth under the faucet and takes in a mouthful of water, swishes, spits it out. She looks like she's ready to collapse. "Just let it go."

"I mean, we're paying him for this. How can you talk to someone like that who's paying you?"

"Would you let it go, Lee? For Christ's sake."

Ellen peers down at the floor. I take a step toward her.

"What," I say.

She looks up, agitated. "What?"

"Just say it."

"Say what?"

"Whatever you're not saying. I can tell. Come on, what is it?"

"It's not the time, Lee." Her voice is like tissue paper, soft and airy and fragile.

"You agree with him? You think I wasn't invested in this thing?"

"You don't invest in things, Lee. You just don't, okay? Yes, I agree with him."

I stumble back a few steps and steady myself against the television. "Don't do that. You can't take our history and apply it to this situation. It's not the same thing at all."

"It's got nothing to do with that. Or maybe it does, I don't know. I can't even tell anymore. You didn't want to hire Walter because you didn't want to hire anyone, because you were too scared of what might happen with Julie. You didn't want to take the chance, you figured, 'Let her stay out there on the farm, it's less trouble for me.'"

"I can't believe you're saying this to me!" I shout, holding my hands up like I'm being mugged at gunpoint. "That's my kid, too, and she's out there right now, and I don't know where she is. I didn't want to hire Walter because I didn't want to jump the fucking gun. You can't throw that in my face. I was being rational. One of us had to be."

"Fuck, Lee! You wanted me to say what I was thinking? This is it. You are terrified, you always have been. The marriage, Julie, this whole intervention thing. You are too fucking terrified to consider anyone's needs but your own."

"You're a psychiatrist now?"

"You asked!"

"So, what is this then? Like, some kind of catharsis for you? Stuff you've been waiting to unload? I hope you feel better, I really do."

"I told you to let it go!"

Bracing myself against the top of the dusty television set, I take a deep and unsteady breath. My eyes are burning, I feel like I could sleep for a week straight, no problem. "What was that all about the other night?" I say after a few seconds. "Why did you come to my room?"

"Jesus, what do you think it was about, Lee? Do you understand how hard this is for me? I needed you to be there for me. I needed, I guess, to feel like we were in this thing together. And, yes, it was a little unfair of me to put you in that situation, and I'm sorry I had to do it, but don't you understand that I'm going out of my mind here, and you haven't made it any easier?"

As I said before, a good salesman needs to be intuitive: he needs to understand people's wants and needs and motivations, and I'm usually pretty adept at this. Ellen, however, was the only person I never learned to read in this way, and it made me both love her and hate her, and it dawns on me now for the first time, sadly, that maybe my failure in this regard, to ever really figure her out, evoked in her a similar set of feelings. How long can you struggle to understand somebody before it hits you that maybe there's nothing to figure out, or at least nothing that can make you love that person in the way you know you're supposed to?

Maybe you're in the wrong business then.

A heavy silence comes over us. Somewhere outside, a dog barks in the distance. "Look," she says in a half-groan, rubbing her temples, "I'm going out to look for her. Just stay here, okay? We can finish talking about this later, but can we please just find her now? Okay?"

I run my hand through my hair. It needs a wash. "Yeah, okay. I'll wait here until she comes back."

"We're just all really, really tired."

"I know," I reply with a shrug, though it's clear that she doesn't really buy this: she just doesn't want to admit to herself that she believes I've failed. But she will, sooner or later.

**

What are the chances of Julie coming back? I mean, do I really foresee her having some inexplicable change of heart and then slogging back here to finish out the intervention?

No, I don't. She knows what's waiting for her here.

And in a strange way, I'm kind of okay with this. If she returns to the Cosmic Brethren compound, then we won't have to worry about where she is. And if she heads off someplace else entirely? Well, at the very least, she'll be free of the Brethren. Right now, that's really the only bright side we've got.

Still, even the most futile endeavors demand a certain degree of faith, and so I'm quite content to wait here in case, by some grand stroke of luck, Julie does in fact return to the motel—except that I'm going on about an hour of sleep at this point and there's no coffee maker in the room, and so I'm going to have to make a quick trip over to the diner for a to-go cup.

Outside the sun is up, hiding behind a curtain of clouds. Most of the rainwater is gone from the parking lot, save for a few puddles cowering in the craggy divots. The rains have left the air heavy and cloying and warm, and I begin to wish that I'd brought a pair of shorts. As I step onto the small gum-encrusted walkway in front of the diner, I'm struck with a poignant sense of finality, like a vacation is coming to an end. You invest enough time and emotion into any place, you'll begin to miss it.

Inside the diner, I spot Phyllis prattling around behind the bar with a dirty white rag slung over her shoulder. She looks up when I enter. "There he is," she says with a slight note of amusement in her voice.

"Here I am"

"Was wondering if we was gonna see you today. You want coffee?"

I'm about to say yes when out of the corner of my eye I notice on the far side of the restaurant a blonde head of hair peeking above one of the broad seatbacks. I stand on my tiptoes and lean forward to get a better look. Phyllis, confused, follows my gaze.

"That's my daughter," I mutter.

"Who, that girl there?"

Without answering, I make my way across the restaurant to Julie. It's all I can do not to break into a dead sprint down the small aisle between the bar and the long row of booths, but I know that I've got to be very careful about this, I don't want to scare her off, and so I move cautiously, as though any moment she may try to bolt.

"Hey, sweetie," I say when I get to the table. I place my hand on her shoulder, just to see what she'll do. When she doesn't move, I lean down and wrap my arms around her shoulders and press my forehead against her ear.

God, am I actually trembling? Indeed I am.

"I tried to go back," she says into her glass, her voice a wasted drone that seems to issue from some place deep inside of her frail body. "I was going to hitchhike back to the compound. But I couldn't."

I take a seat across from her. "Why not?"

Julie shrugs and sips her glass of water. "I don't know. It's like, why bother? There or here, I'm pretty much under house arrest."

"Yeah," I say, more to myself, though I'm not really sure why I'm saying it. The whole thing is a little bit like trying not to divulge some big secret, the way that every spark in my body wants to leap, dance, cartwheel: Julie's here! She came back!

"You guys really screwed me up, you know," she says peevishly. "Kidnapping me and all. Keeping me hostage." She's trying her best to sound pissed off, but her heart's no longer in it. Which phase of recovery are we in now? I want to grab her, pull her to me, smell her head.

"Honey, I'm so sorry. I really am. But you have to understand what we were trying to do. I mean, it killed us, your mother and me, to see what was happening to you."

"So, what was happening to me?"

It's a tricky question, one with an agenda; she's looking to me to tell her how she's supposed to feel about this whole thing. And I very much want to, because I'm her father, and I should be able to fix things for my kid. But it's more complicated than that. How is anyone who's gone through what we've been through supposed to feel?

After thinking it over for a few seconds, I say, "You were turning into someone else, a different person. We didn't recognize you. And it scared us."

Phyllis appears and refills Julie's cup from a plastic water pitcher. "You want some coffee?" the woman asks me.

The plainness of the question throws me: Do I want some coffee, yes or no? "Yes, please. Some coffee would be great," I finally stammer. She disappears and returns with a steaming pot of coffee and a mug. "How's the trip?" she says as she pours.

"Winding down," I reply. "We're heading home today."

"Well, that'll be good, I guess," she says indifferently, glancing over at Julie every few seconds.

"This is my daughter Julie," I say to her.

"Ah," says Phyllis. She gives Julie a friendly nod and smiles. "Good to meet you."

Julie smiles timidly and says thank you, her eyes barely leaving her plate. Phyllis asks us if we want anything to eat. Julie shakes her head, but I order a plate of orange slices anyway. Just to have something on the table.

When Phyllis is gone, I give Julie a sheepish smile. "That's Phyllis," I say.

Julie giggles soundlessly. "You made a friend."

"Indeed I did."

She looks out the window, seeming to study the road for a moment, and then turns back to me. "Look, can we just sit here for a little while?" she says, folding her arms on the table. "I mean, not long, just a little bit. Would that be okay? We can, like, just sit and have coffee?"

I reach across the table and take her hand. It is hard and coarse from working in the orchards, the pads of her tiny fingers like scar tissue. It's the hand of someone with a history, someone with a story to tell. Smiling, I tell her, "As long as you need."

This book would not have been possible without the support and guidance of the following:

Linda & Dixie Griffin, Karen Luurtsema (& her fifth period chem class), Ed Falco, Weston Cutter, Carrie Meadows, Nick Kocz, Lucinda Roy, Jeff Mann, Fred D'Aguiar, the Virginia Tech Creative Writing Department, Tim Lockridge, Paul Heilker, Neil Norman, Sally Boman, Aileen Murphy, Mark Spewak & Liz Grant-Spewak, Vince Daus & Meika Fields, Brice Harrington & Maggie Waggoner, Phil Waltz, Brian Shiplov & Kelly Erickson-Shiplov, Jeff Lodge, Michelle Dexter, Kimberly Verhines, SFASU Press, Laura Valeri, the Starbucks of Christiansburg, VA, Alix Ohlin, Steve Almond, John Simoneaux, Beth Ashburn, The Virginia Military Institute Department of English and Fine Arts, and of course my students.